DEBORAH GOES TO DOVER

Being the Fifth Volume of the Travelling Matchmaker

M.C. Beaton

CHIVERS

British Library Cataloguing in Publication Data available

First published in the UK by Robinson, an imprint
of Constable & Robinson Ltd, 2011.
This Large Print edition published by AudioGO Ltd, Bath, 2012.
Published by arrangement with Constable & Robinson Ltd.

U.K.   Hardcover   ISBN   978 14458 3800 7
U.K.   Softcover   ISBN   978 14458 3801 4

Copyright © M.C. Beaton 1992

The right of M.C. Beaton to be identified as the author of this work has
been asserted by her in accordance with the Copyright, Designs and
Patents Act, 1988

Printed and bound in Great Britain by
MPG Books Group Limited

The author warns readers not on any account to try any of the cosmetic recipes in this book.

1

Love that comes too late,
Like a remorseful pardon slowly carried.
William Shakespeare

Miss Hannah Pym was in love.

She had fancied herself in love a long time ago when she had still been a servant, rather than the gentlewoman of independent means she was now. But this, she realized, was actually love at last. The real thing.

Not the flowery hopeful love of sweet sixteen, but middle-aged love, hopeless love, yearning bordered with black despair.

Hannah was in her forties. The object of her affections was a bachelor in his fifties. Nothing, on the face of it, could have been more suitable. But the object of her affections was none other than Sir George Clarence, brother of her late employer, the employer who had left her a legacy in his will and therefore enabled her to say goodbye to her days of servitude. That had been at the beginning of the year, this brand-new year of 1800.

She had used some of the money to go on four journeys in the Flying Machines, as the stage-coaches were called, and had acquired a faithful footman, Benjamin, and the friendship of Sir George.

But that friendship showed no sign of blossoming into anything warmer. When she had returned from her last expedition, to Brighton, Hannah had suffered a blow. Sir George had been on the point of proposing to a Miss Bearcroft. When Miss Bearcroft had been unmasked as a lady of doubtful reputation, Sir George had retreated, feeling himself lucky not to have made a terrible mistake, but the very fact that he had proved himself to be so vulnerable to the opposite sex had struck Hannah like a hammer-blow. Instead of giving her hope, it had given her gloomy thoughts of a Sir George susceptible to the next doubtful charmer who set her cap at him.

These dismal thoughts were going through her head as she waited in the yard of the Spread Eagle in Gracechurch Street for the Dover coach. Should she have stayed in London rather than taking the pain of her newfound love off to the English coast? And yet Sir George enjoyed hearing about her adventures, and how could Hannah Pym have any adventures to tell him if she ceased her travels?

The coach, the *Tally-Ho,* was brought round into the yard. Benjamin helped the guard stow their luggage in the basket, assisted Hannah in boarding the coach, and then climbed up onto the roof to take his seat with the outsiders.

Hannah was the first passenger on the

inside. She wondered vaguely what the other passengers would be like, but without any of her normal sharp interest. She had already brought about several successful matches between couples she had met on her travels, but a lady who now desires more than anything else in the world to be married herself cannot turn her mind to other people's romances. Hannah decided to mind her own business and try to enjoy the scenery and think up descriptions to tell Sir George: Sir George of the piercing blue eyes and silver-white hair.

One by one, the other passengers began to board the coach. There was an army captain, a grim-faced man, wearing his pigtail and scarlet regimentals; a plain young lady, in a depressing bonnet, guarded by what appeared to be her mother; and an elderly clergyman and his mousy wife. A dull lot, thought Hannah uncharitably.

The hour was six in the morning and an angry dawn was rising above the jumbled chimneys of the City of London. A high wind was blowing and the cowls on the chimney-pots spun round and round, sending snakes of grey smoke down into the streets.

The coach was to go to Dover by Rochester, Sittingbourne, Ospringe and Canterbury. It rumbled its way through London and down through the turnpike at New Cross. From there, under increasingly black and threatening skies, it made its way to Deptford;

Deptford, where in 1581 Queen Elizabeth went on board Drake's ship, the *Golden Hind*, in which the greatest of English seamen had circumnavigated the globe. On board the *Golden Hind* the queen dined, and after dinner knighted the captain. Twelve years after this famous dinner, the playwright Christopher Marlowe was killed at Deptford at the age of twenty-nine in a tavern brawl.

Immediately beyond Deptford, they began to travel across Blackheath. Hannah, who had read many history books and guidebooks, recollected that it was at Blackheath in 1381 that Wat Tyler had marshalled his one hundred thousand rebels. That other rebel, Lord Audley, had also gathered his troops at Blackheath, having brought them all the way from Cornwall, and he had suffered a defeat immediately afterwards by Henry VII.

Blackheath was full of memories of kings and queens. In 1400, Henry IV met Manuel, Emperor of Constantinople. Henry V, after a long triumphal procession from Dover, was met on Blackheath by the mayor and five hundred citizens of London. And it was on Blackheath that the already much-married Henry VIII received his fourth wife, Anne of Cleves, and on Blackheath where the crowds cried, 'Long live King Charles!' as the restored Charles II rose between his brothers, the Dukes of York and Gloucester.

Hannah brought her thoughts back to the

present when the coach finally rolled into the yard of the Bull at Dartford, where the passengers were to breakfast. It was a fine old galleried inn. From the archway hung a veritable forest of game, banging into the faces of the outsiders on the roof as the coach swept underneath.

Hannah climbed stiffly down. For the first time she could ever remember, she felt vaguely unwell and wondered if love, like a sickness, ate into one's very bones.

She found herself the focus of interested attention because of Benjamin, her footman, who stood punctiliously behind her chair, dressed in black-and-gold livery. Hannah felt uneasy every time she thought about that livery. Benjamin had bought it in Brighton and she knew he had purchased it with his winnings from gambling. For the hundredth time Hannah thought she really must do something about Benjamin's gambling. What if he were to lose heavily and she had to pay his debts? Her legacy of five thousand pounds had seemed such a fortune a short time ago, before she moved up in the world, away from her little room above the bakery in Kensington to her now smart and fashionable apartment in the heart of London's West End. Admittedly, thanks to Benjamin, she had not had to dig very deep into it, for the enterprising footman always seemed to have a supply of ready money from gambling for coals and candles and food.

Hannah's conscience stabbed her. She was living off his earnings, *immoral* earnings, she told herself severely.

The breakfast was superb. Hannah dismissed Benjamin, who went to take his own meal with the coachman and guard. She glanced across the room and stiffened in shock. There was a large mirror over the sideboard and she saw her own reflection clearly.

Now Hannah, like a lot of middle-aged ladies, hardly ever looked at herself closely in the glass, preferring to carry about with her a manufactured picture of her own appearance. But there she was, the real Hannah Pym, fortyish and spinsterish from her flat-chested, spare figure to her sandy hair and crooked nose. Her only beauty lay in her eyes, which were like opals and changed colour according to her mood.

How, thought Hannah bitterly, could she ever expect the handsome and distinguished Sir George Clarence to become enamoured of such as she?

'Have you had a Spasm?' asked a voice next to her. Hannah controlled her features and turned to face her companion, the mother of the young girl on the coach. 'I am very well, I thank you,' said Hannah politely.

'I am Mrs Conningham,' said the lady, 'and this is my daughter, Abigail.'

The young lady, Abigail, threw Hannah

a tentative smile. Warmed by good food, the passengers began to relax. The soldier turned out to be a Captain Beltravers, and the clergyman, a non-conformist minister called Mr Osborne, introduced his wife, who blushed furiously at having to speak to anyone at all.

Hannah began to revive. Her interest in her fellow passengers sharpened. As long as one could be interested in people and their problems, then one could manage to ignore one's own, thought Hannah. 'Are we all going as far as Dover?' she asked.

Mrs Conningham, her daughter, and the captain were all going the full length of the journey, but the clergyman and his wife were leaving the coach at Rochester.

Hannah wondered why Miss Abigail Conningham looked so sad. She might not look so very plain if she were happy, thought Hannah. As it was, her little face was white and pinched, and her eyes looked very small, although there was a suspicious puffiness about them as if she had been weeping. And why did the captain look so grim and old? Studying him, Hannah reflected he must be only in his early thirties, and that was followed by a sharp pang of memory of the days gone by when Hannah Pym would have regarded anyone in his thirties as old.

She asked Abigail whether she were still at school and Abigail answered shyly that she had left a seminary in Chiswick over three years ago. Hannah judged her to be twenty, older than she had first thought. 'And what takes you to Dover?' asked Hannah, her eyes turning green with curiosity.

'My uncle resides there,' said Abigail bleakly. 'We are to live with him.'

Her mother threw her a warning look and she subsided into miserable silence.

When they boarded the coach again, the heavens opened and the rain came down, steel rods of rain, drumming on the roof and cascading across the glass. Hannah hoped her footman would not catch the ague. There was no let-up in the rain. From Dartford, they ploughed through Gravesend and so towards Rochester. The inside of the coach was damp and cold, and the passengers shivered and wondered if the rain would ever stop.

Hannah thought of her previous adventures and reflected gloomily there would be nothing to tell Sir George about this journey except a tale of damp and discomfort. There was no handsome aristocrat, no pretty heroine, nothing but a grim captain and a plain, sad girl. But there was one beautiful lady shortly about to cross Hannah's path, although if Hannah had seen her at that moment, she would have doubted very much if a match could be made for such a creature.

*   *   *

Lady Deborah Western looked out at the pouring rain, yawned, and swung her booted feet, which had been resting on a console table, down onto the floor.

'Damned flat, ain't it?' she said to her brother.

Lady Deborah and her brother were twins. Often they were mistaken for brothers, for Lady Deborah affected men's clothes. Her golden curls were cut short and she had the same firm jaw and straight nose as her brother and the same large blue eyes. Their father, the Earl of Staye, was off on his travels again, Turkey this time. The countess had died giving birth to the twins, and they had looked after each other from the day they were both old enough to toddle and begin their career of routing any servant from nursery maid to governess who tried to thwart them. They hunted, rode and shot and fished together, recently with an added pleasure, for their father had threatened that the next time he returned, Deborah was to be presented at her first Season and brother William was to join a regiment, although neither could quite believe their indulgent parent would carry out such a dreadful threat.

'Have you heard that Ashton's back from the wars?' asked Lord William, taking a sugarplum from a box and tossing it to a mangy wolfhound who was lying on one of the drawing-room sofas.

9

'What!' Lady Deborah looked interested. 'Not Puritan Ashton?'

'Yes, returned from the wars to take up the title and do something with that crumbling family barn on the other side of Rochester.'

'He'll have enough money,' said Lady Deborah. 'The old earl never spent a penny if he could help it. Left a fortune.'

'Don't envy him the task of putting his place in order all the same,' commented William idly. 'He'll be in his thirties now.' He looked at his sister slyly. 'You know Papa has hopes for you in that direction.'

'Pooh! Ashton's too old,' said the nineteen-year-old Lady Deborah. 'I remember him. How old were we when he came here? Ten or eleven? And he told Papa a good thrashing was what we both needed.'

'You put mice in his best boots,' said her brother reflectively. 'Wasn't he mad!'

'And stuffy,' said Deborah, wrinkling her nose. 'Do you remember what he said to Papa? "You cannot let these children run wild and behave any way they like or they will grow up to be monsters."'

'And he was right,' said William with a grin. 'You must admit, Deborah, you're a sadly unnatural female, wearing men's clothes and hunting and shooting. You'll have the dowagers at Almack's fainting with horror.'

'I am not going to Almack's. I can always talk Papa round,' said Lady Deborah. 'Why should he bother? I don't need a rich husband. We have plenty of money. I like it here.' She looked happily around the cluttered drawing-room, full of discarded books, game bags, fishing poles and guns.

She loved their home, Downs Abbey, with its dark old rooms and twisting corridors and smoking fires. The drawing-room looked out on a prospect of green parkland and ornamental lake. The earl employed an excellent head gardener. Despite their careless ways, the twins helped the estates manager to see that everything was in order when their father was away, and knew as much about the running of the estates as he did himself.

'Mind you, Papa could have a point,' said Lord William lazily. 'Was down at the Crown in Rochester t'other night. Ball going on in the assembly rooms. Had a peek. Some real dazzlers, all in the latest fashions.' He waved his arms. 'Dainty muslins and things. You don't half look a guy, sometimes, Deborah.'

Lady Deborah looked hurt. 'You never complained before.'

'I know. But have you ever thought I might like to woo some little charmer? What if I bring her and her mama here and introduce them to you? You'd frighten them off.'

'Why are you being so cruel!' exclaimed Deborah, appalled at this new idea of a brother who would leave her, and that one day she would take very second place to a wife.

He stood up and began to pace up and down. 'Sorry,' he said. 'It's the demned rain. Will it never stop?'

* * *

The Earl of Ashton stood by the fireplace in his library, frowning down at a letter he had just received. It was from the Earl of Staye. It congratulated him on inheriting the title and commiserated with him on his father's death. Very polite and formal. But it was the last paragraph that made the Earl of Ashton's mouth curl in distaste. 'I would be grateful if you would call on my son and daughter. I fear Deborah is a trifle hoydenish and she and William run wild. Pray see that they do not get into mischief while I am gone. I comfort myself with the thought it is not too onerous a task for you in view of the fact we are neighbours.'

The Earl of Staye's place, Downs Abbey, lay a good thirty-five miles away across bad roads.

The Earl of Ashton tossed the letter in the fire. He had no intention of making the journey to Downs Abbey until the weather cleared and the roads improved. How old would the twins be now? Nineteen? Too old and too used to their own rough ways to want any advice from him.

He shivered slightly despite the warmth of the fire. The library smelt damp. Ashton Park had been built early in the seventeenth century and nothing much had been done to it since then. An elderly footman tottered in carrying a tray which held a coffee-pot and cup and, with shaking hands, deposited it gingerly on a low table before backing out.

Although he had assured the old servants that they could all keep their jobs or retire on generous pensions, they all seemed afraid of him and he wondered why. He had always prided himself on being honest, generous and fair, and he knew the men in his old regiment had found no fault with his command.

He did not know that it was his appearance which had frightened the servants so much, the servants who had not seen him for a longtime. He was tall, very tall and lithe, and hard-featured with green eyes and a proud nose. His hair was jet-black and his eyebrows flew upwards. It was the cook who had started the fuss by crossing herself and saying the devil had taken possession of the new earl's soul. The gossip had grown among the servants. One said that before he went to the wars, the earl's eyes had been as blue as the sea and his hair brown. This was untrue, but it made a good story to shiver and tremble over in the servants' hall. Besides, there was a certain *cachet* in having a master who was rumoured to be the devil, and so the servants, having begun by frightening themselves more for the fun of it than anything else, actually became very frightened of their master indeed, as fiction took the place of fact in their elderly minds.

Some of the earl's friends, who would have said that his only faults were that he was apt to be too pompous and strict, almost righteous, would have been highly amused at his new reputation.

*   *   *

Hannah wrapped her cloak tightly about her for warmth. The coach was lurching from side to side, travelling now at a crazy speed as if the coachman were trying to outrun the pouring rain. Captain Beltravers put his head out of the window to shout to the coachman to be careful and got a flood of rainwater in his face for his pains.

'He'll have us in the ditch!' said Mr Osborne, and his wife let out a shrill scream and clutched at him for support.

On and on they thundered. Surely they should be near Rochester and sanctuary. Each thought of a warm inn and a roaring fire.

And then the inevitable happened. The coachman, sure that he had nothing but a good stretch of empty road in front of him, fanned his horses. He raised his sleeve to wipe the rain from his eyes and suddenly in front of him loomed the up coach from Dover. The horses swerved wildly and the *Tally-Ho*'s wheels got caught in a deep ditch. With a great cracking sound, the whole coach went over on its side, throwing the passengers, coachman and guard off the top of the coach and leaving the inside passengers piled one on top of the other.

The guard on the up coach blew a cheeky tootle on his horn and left the stricken *Tally-Ho* to its fate.

The inside passengers were battered and bruised but no bones had been broken. The outsiders had been thrown clear onto springy heath and had also survived without much mishap. Their angry voices berating the coachman reached the ears of the insiders as they struggled to disentangle themselves. Then they were all mixed up again as the outsiders, guard and coachman, having cut the plunging horses free, pushed the coach upright again.

Hannah banged her head on the floor and tried to push Mr Osborne from on top of her. Mrs Osborne was screaming like a banshee and Mrs Conningham had fainted.

When they were all finally back in their seats and Hannah had revived Mrs Conningham by putting her ever-ready vinaigrette under that lady's nose, the door was opened and the outsiders tried to climb in to take shelter from the rain. But much as Hannah would have liked to shelter Benjamin, the rest protested violently. The outsiders had paid for outsiders' places and were wet anyway. Let them stay outside!

Benjamin poked his head through the

window to tell Hannah that the guard had ridden off to Rochester, a mile away, to get help.

'We'll never reach Dover alive at this rate,' said Mrs Conningham. Hannah thought she heard Abigail whisper, 'Good', and despite her own discomfort, Hannah's interest was revived. What was there about this visit to her uncle's which so obviously depressed poor Abigail?

After an hour of shivering and trying to keep warm and talking in miserable whispers, as if the rain would hear them and never go away, the coach door opened and the coachman said proudly, just as if he had not nearly killed them all, that the landlord of the Crown at Rochester had sent carriages to convey them to the inn.

Hannah stepped down into the rain-swept landscape. She was very cold indeed and her head had begun to ache. She gratefully accepted Benjamin's arm and allowed him to assist her to one of the carriages from the inn. Benjamin climbed in after her, saying, 'I ain't walking. There's room enough for all of us.'

'Poor Benjamin,' said Hannah contritely. 'Servant or not, you should have been travelling inside with me. Your livery must be ruined. You should have had a greatcoat.'

'It's this poxy English weather, modom,' said Benjamin gloomily. 'Warn't it lovely and fine the day afore we left?' His clever mobile face looked like that of a sad clown. Water was running from his powdered hair, and the shoulders of his black velvet livery were being covered in a sort of Yorkshire pudding of water and flour.

Rooms at the Crown had been reserved for the shattered passengers, with the exception of Mr Osborne and his wife, who had reached their destination and left for their home, Mr Osborne threatening to sue the stage-coach company.

Hannah shivered as she removed her bonnet and then set about changing her clothes. Her head felt hot and heavy and her vision was blurred. She made her way down to the dining-room. Benjamin looked at her sharply and said, 'Anything amiss, modom? You're as red as a lobster.'

'I shall come about,' said Hannah vaguely. She was very hungry, but as soon as the excellent meal was placed in front of her, her appetite seemed to flee. She gave an involuntary shiver and stared at her food.

Benjamin, standing behind her chair, leaned forward. 'It's off to bed for you,' he whispered fiercely. 'Come along!'

Hannah meekly allowed her footman to lead her upstairs. 'Get into your night-clothes,' ordered Benjamin, stirring up the fire. When he had left, Hannah undressed in a daze, put on a night-dress, tied on her nightcap and climbed stiffly into bed. The next thing she was aware of was Benjamin's anxious face swimming in front of her through a sort of red mist and his voice telling her the doctor was on his way.

Hannah lay in the grip of a raging fever for two days, nursed by Benjamin. During the middle of the second night, her fever broke and she fell into a deep refreshing sleep. When she awoke, Benjamin was there to give her newspapers, novels, and a basket of fruit. 'You are a good boy,' said Hannah feebly. 'Fetch my reticule and I will give you some money.'

Benjamin hesitated and then said lightly, 'I already took the money from you, modom, you being too ill to know anythink.'

So Hannah rested and read and was brought light meals by the inn waiters during the rest of that day. The only thing to worry her as she blew out her candle at night was that Benjamin had mysteriously disappeared and that he had lied about taking money from her reticule, for he had taken none at all.

The next day, she felt almost well, but worried. There was still no Benjamin. The inn servants said they had not seen him and his bed had not been slept in.

Early that evening, she received a visit from Mrs and Miss Conningham and Captain Beltravers. They said the roads were still bad after the downpour and they would be obliged to stay at the inn for a few more days but that the coach company was expected to pay for everything. Hannah asked them if they had seen her footman, but they shook their heads.

Hannah was just deciding to try to read herself to sleep when there came a scratching at the door and the captain walked in. 'I could see you were worried about your footman,' he said, taking a chair and placing it beside the bed and sitting down.

'Have you news?' asked Hannah eagerly.

'I have debated with myself whether to tell you or not, whether to leave you to worry about his absence, or to worry you with what has happened.'

Hannah struggled up against the pillows. 'Oh, do tell me, Captain. You must tell me now. I have it. He has been gambling.'

'So I have heard. There was to be a prize-fight here tomorrow and the town is full of the Quality. Randall was to fight Chudd, but Chudd is ill and unless a substitute is found, the fight will be off. But meanwhile, all the Fancy are in town with money to burn. Your footman got into a game of hazard dice and the stakes were high. He lost.'

'How much?' asked Hannah.

'Nine hundred guineas.'

'But he cannot possibly afford that!'

'Which may be the reason,' said the captain, 'that he has disappeared.'

'He would not,' said Hannah. 'He would see me first. He must know I would always help him.'

'If he is the hardened gambler he appears to be,' commented the captain drily, 'then you would be throwing good money after bad.'

After Captain Beltravers had gone, Hannah lay and thought about Benjamin. She knew if he had really gone away that she would miss him dreadfully, miss his cheeky good humour and his loyalty. She still felt weak and a large tear rolled down her thin sallow cheek.

*　　　*　　　*

Lady Deborah struggled awake the next morning to find her brother shaking her. 'What's amiss?' she demanded crossly.

'That fight, it's still on,' he said. 'You've always wanted to see a prize-fight. Now's your chance. Get dressed.'

Lady Deborah's blue eyes gleamed with excitement. 'Who is fighting Randall?'

'Some unknown.'

'Brave man! You said Randall was a killer.'

'If this unknown beats him, he stands to gain a purse of a thousand guineas. Hurry up. It's on Gully's Field and if we don't move quickly, the roads will be jammed in every direction.'

*　　　*　　　*

The Earl of Ashton was also roused early by the arrival of an old army friend, Mr

Peter Carruthers. 'What brings you here, Carruthers?' asked the earl. 'Not that I am not delighted to see you.'

'You're really out of the world,' said Mr Carruthers with a grin. 'A prize-fight. A mill. And nearly on your own doorstep.'

'Who is fighting whom?'

'Randall was supposed to be fighting Chudd, but Chudd is ill, or so he said, and some unknown has stepped into the breach.'

'More fool he,' commented the earl. 'Do you really think it worth the effort of watching a possible amateur be massacred by Randall?'

'If it turns out to be bad sport, we can always leave,' pointed out Mr Carruthers.

The earl decided to go, more because he found to his surprise that he had been lonely and was sick of his own company. Peter Carruthers was a tall, lanky, easy-going fellow and just the sort of company the earl felt he needed. The sun was shining and he wondered for a brief moment whether he ought not to ride to Downs Abbey to see how those spoilt brats of Staye's were surviving, but in the next moment, decided against it. Soon he and Mr Carruthers joined all the other carriages making their way to Gully's Field outside Rochester.

*   *   *

Hannah Pym arose early and went out into the cobbled, rain-washed streets of the old town of Rochester. She had not had breakfast. She did not feel like eating. She planned to walk about the town, just to see if she could find any clue to Benjamin's whereabouts. The sum he had lost would take a great chunk out of her inheritance, and though she cursed Benjamin in her heart for his gambling, she knew she would gladly pay it to get him back again.

The town was full of bustle and noise and carriages. The prize-fight, Hannah remembered. How gentlemen could find pleasure in watching two men beating each other to a pulp was beyond her. She searched and searched, asking for news of Benjamin in inns and taverns. The town began to empty and wear a deserted air as all the carriages bearing the prize-fight enthusiasts rattled off.

Shabby men and women had been going around the streets handing out what looked like playbills. One fluttered along the street and caught on Hannah's skirt. She plucked it off impatiently and was about to toss it away when the cheap black lettering on it leaped up at her.

'Mr George Randall, Pugilist Supreme, to fight Mr Benjamin Stubbs, the London Gentleman.'

Her heart in her mouth, she read on. The fight was to take place at ten o'clock that morning in a place called Gully's Field. She

22

glanced at the watch pinned to her bosom. Eight o'clock. If she had asked for a footman called Benjamin Stubbs, someone might have put her wise earlier, but all she had done was give a description of the missing Benjamin, not his name. She asked back at the inn for directions to Gully's Field and learned it was six miles off to the north of the town. Hannah knew she had no hope of hiring any sort of carriage or even farm cart, as every vehicle in the vicinity would have been taken up. Setting her lips in a grim line, and holding a serviceable umbrella like a club in one hand, she set out walking the long road to Gully's Field.

2

If thou love game at so dear a rate,
Learn this, that hath old gamesters dearly cost:
Dost lose? rise up: dost win? rise in that state,
Who strive to sit out losing hands are lost.
George Herbert

Boxing had reached the zenith of its popularity. Patronized as it was by royalty, nobles and commoners alike, a prize match could bring thousands flocking to the scene.

Lady Deborah Western was beginning to feel a trifle uneasy, but glad she was wearing men's clothes. Any lady attending such an affair would surely cause a scandal. She and her brother were fortunate that they had arrived early enough to secure a place for their carriage at the ringside. By the time the fight was due to begin, the carriages were ten deep around the ring and thousands of foot spectators were spread up the sloping hillsides round about which turned the field into a natural amphitheatre.

All about Lady Deborah, voices loud in boxing cant traded their knowledge. The odds were stated in quaint terms. It was, 'Chelsea Hospital to a sentry-box on Randall,' or 'Glass case of '51 to a cucumber frame on the unknown.' The faces of the boxing heroes were frontispieces or dial-plates; their mouths, potato traps, gin-traps, kissers, or ivory-boxes; their heads, nuts, nobs or knowledge boxes; their blood, currant juice or claret; their eyes, ogles or optics; their stomachs, bread-baskets or victualling offices; and their noses, conks, snouts or smellers.

Even the newspaper reports were written in cant. Lord William had shown his sister a report of a prize-fight which described the arrival of the boxers as, 'The men came to the scratch, with good-humour painted on their mugs.'

Then Lady Deborah noticed a movement and fuss about the shabby carriage next to her. The man at the reins seemed to be about

24

to move off. Wondering that anyone, having secured such a prime place, should forgo it, she watched in surprise. Just as he was ready to drive off, a smart racing curricle with two men in it drove right across the ring. The stewards held up the ropes. The carriage next to her drove off and its place was taken by the curricle.

'Clever way to secure a good place, Carruthers,' said one of the newcomers.

'Oh, Parsons is a good fellow,' replied the man called Carruthers. 'I paid him well to be here early so that we should get the best view.'

Lady Deborah eyed Carruthers's companion and she jogged her brother with her elbow. 'Ain't that old Puritan Ashton in beside us?'

Lord William looked across her and hissed in dismay. 'Sure it is,' he whispered. 'Looks like the devil, don't he? I remember those green eyes of his. Pull your hat down over your eyes, Deb. If he recognizes you, he'll give you a jaw-me-dead and spoil our fun.'

Mr Peter Carruthers took out his quizzing-glass and looked about. He studied the twins in the next carriage. 'Beautiful pair of lads,' he commented, 'although the one near you is a trifle girlish. Could do with toughening up.'

The Earl of Ashton looked at the pair just described. His face hardened. 'That, my dear friend,' he said loudly, 'is none other than Lord William Western and his sister, Lady Deborah.

The young whelp has dressed his sister in his clothes and brought her to a prize-fight.'

His voice carried to the other spectators hard by and Deborah suddenly found herself the focus of much attention, followed by loud taunts. A pair of fine legs in skin-tight breeches occasion no comment when supposed to belong to a man, but when it is revealed the delectable limbs are those of a lady, coarse remarks are apt to rise all round. To Deborah's burning ears came lubricious suggestions about where the gentlemen would like to find those legs—tight around their necks being the general and loud opinion.

She felt tears of mortification rising to her eyes. If only the fight would start so that her tormentors would leave her alone. She cursed Lord Ashton. She felt sure he had revealed her identity quite deliberately. Lord William was almost as miserable. He could not call them all out for insulting his sister. He was made even more miserable by the knowledge that he and his friends would no doubt bait any lady just as much had she attended a prize-fight dressed like a man. There was no way they could retreat until the fight was over.

And then, to Lady Deborah's relief, a hush fell on the crowd as the two fighters walked into the ring. Then there was an outcry. For the champion, Randall, was all that a champion should be, squat and powerful with a Neanderthal jaw, but the unknown, Benjamin

Stubbs, was tall and slim. The odds rose high in favour of the champion.

'My money's on Randall, and so is everyone else's,' said Mr Carruthers gloomily.

'I think I shall back our unknown,' said the earl. 'But let's see how he strips.'

Benjamin removed his coat and handed it to his second and that was followed by his ruffled shirt. His chest was white and hairless and his arms were sinewy, but he cut a poor figure beside Randall, who had a mat of hair on his chest like a carriage rug and whose arms were as thick as tree trunks.

'Not much sport today,' said Lord William, leaning forward, and Lady Deborah heaved a sigh of relief and prayed it would all be over quickly.

It was a beautiful morning, clear and still, with a delicate fuzz of new green leaves covering the trees on the hills above the ring. Great fluffy clouds sailed across a clear blue sky and the air was warm and sweet.

The contestants squared up to each other, the handkerchief was dropped and they set to. The couple sparred for a few minutes. There was deathly silence. Then Randall, moving with amazing speed for so heavily built a man, put two dextrous hits through Benjamin's guard, hitting him in the mouth and the throat at the same minute. Benjamin fell like a log, covered with blood, as cheer after cheer for Randall rent the air.

27

Lady Deborah closed her eyes and prayed she was not going to be sick.

Benjamin had been sponged down and was squaring up gamely for round two when a woman could be heard shouting from somewhere behind in the crowd. Painfully glad there was at least one other female present, Lady Deborah opened her eyes, only to see Randall punch Benjamin on the side of the head and send him reeling.

And then a middle-aged woman carrying a large umbrella erupted into the ring like a fury. She marched straight up to Randall and brought her umbrella down on his head with a resounding *thwack*. Hannah Pym had arrived.

Her umbrella dated from the last century. It had an oilskin covering, heavy iron spokes, and a silver head in the shape of a grinning dog.

The Earl of Ashton ran lightly into the ring and approached the group of gesticulating stewards who had gathered around Hannah and the fighters.

'Leave my footman alone, you great bully,' howled Hannah.

'It's all right, modom,' said Benjamin. 'I said I was going to fight. No one pressed me into it.'

'You had better come with me,' said Lord Ashton. 'You cannot stop a prize-fight or there will be a riot and many people might be killed.'

'Yes, please go,' said Benjamin. 'Ain't nothing you can do now.'

Hannah looked around wildly. Lord Ashton took her gently by the arm. 'There is a lady in the carriage next to mine,' he said. 'I suggest you join her.'

Lady Deborah watched them approach. Lord Ashton came right up to her and said, 'Since you have had the temerity, the folly, to appear here, the least you can do is offer some protection to this lady.'

Too mortified to do other than make room between herself and William for Hannah, Lady Deborah then sat very still, staring straight ahead.

'He will be killed,' said Miss Hannah Pym. 'I know it.'

'Your son, ma'am?' asked Lady Deborah, finding her voice.

'No,' said Hannah crossly, 'my footman, and as Benjamin is in his thirties and I in my forties, I am tired of people asking me whether he is my son. He is a silly footman who lost a great deal of money gambling and this is his stupid, stupid, dangerous way of trying to recoup his losses. Why are you dressed like a man?'

'Mind your own business, madam, and watch the fight,' said Deborah tartly.

'I do not want to watch the fight,' replied Hannah. 'I do not enjoy public hangings, nor do I like to see public murder done, which is all that a prize-fight is.'

'How long do these . . . these . . . *things*

29

usually go on for?' Deborah asked William.

'Twenty-eight rounds,' he said cheerfully. 'Stubbs has a great deal of bottom and is shaping up well.'

Deborah thought gloomily that Stubbs was going to end up, if he lived, looking like a sort of black-and-blue jelly for the rest of his life.

Benjamin's pluck against such a formidable adversary had caught the crowd's imagination. They began to roar his name, not Stubbs, not the surname which would have been usual, but a huge chant of, 'Benjamin, Benjamin, BENJAMIN!' The noise seemed to galvanize Benjamin, who began to place his punches more accurately. The rounds were mercifully short but by the time the fight reached its fifteenth, Deborah, forgetting Miss Pym was a stranger, was clutching her for support and Hannah had a comforting arm around the girl's shoulders.

At the sixteenth round, Hannah's nerve broke. Freeing herself from Lady Deborah, she jumped to her feet and shouted, 'I cannot stand it any more, Benjamin.'

Benjamin's eyes flickered in her direction. He dived under Randall's guard and landed a massive blow under Randall's ear, that magic spot, as it was described by the boxing expert of the time, Captain Godfrey.

Randall fell like a stone and lay still.

Crying with relief, Hannah cheered and jumped up and down. Deborah leaped to her feet and she and William clung on to Hannah and shouted themselves hoarse.

Benjamin was borne off in triumph from the field. The Earl of Ashton jumped down from his curricle and came up to Deborah. 'I shall call on you later,' he said.

Deborah sank down on the carriage seat. 'Your guardian?' asked Hannah.

Deborah shook her head. 'Only a neighbour.'

'May as well sit here for a bit,' said William. 'There'll be such a press of carriages on the road to Rochester, it would take us ages inching along to get there if we left now.'

A man passed their carriage and leered up at Deborah. 'Holloa, slut-face, show us yer twat,' he jeered. Hannah's ever-ready umbrella came crashing down on his head and he reeled away.

Overcome at last, Deborah began to cry. Although she had hunted and fished in men's clothes and ridden about the countryside in them, she had never appeared in the town with them on, never had worn them anywhere where she might be held up to ridicule. She had been confident all the same that everyone at the fight would assume her to be a man and was sure they might have done so had not the Earl of Ashton betrayed her.

'I h-hate him,' she sobbed.

'Who?' asked Hannah. 'That devilish-looking man?'

'He's the Earl of Ashton and a stuffed shirt if ever there was one,' said William gloomily. 'Don't cry, sis. You'd better dry your eyes and introduce yourself. I am Lord William Western and this is my sister, Deborah.'

'And I am Miss Hannah Pym,' said Hannah, holding out her hand.

He shook it and then said, 'You'd best come home with us for a bit, Miss Pym. Are you living in Rochester?'

'I am residing at the Crown,' said Hannah. 'I am travelling by stage-coach to Dover, but there was an accident to the coach.'

'If we go to our home, Downs Abbey,' pursued William, 'then we will be able to cut across country and avoid the main roads. Then, when all is quiet, I will escort you to Rochester.'

'What of my footman?' asked Hannah.

'He'll have a right royal time being fêted and paraded all about the town.' William looked at her curiously. 'With a purse of a thousand guineas, he may not wish to remain a servant.'

'We'll see,' said Hannah. She put a comforting arm around Deborah's still shaking shoulders. 'Drive on.'

Hannah looked at Downs Abbey with pleasure when they eventually came to a stop in front of it. It was a jumble of various periods of architecture blended by ivy and age into a harmonious whole. A groom came running

32

from the stables to take horses and carriage away and an elderly butler opened the door to the twins and Hannah.

'Tea in the drawing-room, Silvers,' ordered William.

'I must change,' said Deborah. She was much recovered but still looking rather pale. 'I shall join you in a trice.'

In the drawing-room, William shovelled a pile of newspapers and magazines off an armchair and assisted Hannah into it. Hannah gazed about the room. It looked more like the study of two bachelors than a drawing-room, she reflected. There was a mangy wolfhound taking up most of the sofa and two spaniels lay stretched out before the fire.

The butler and two footmen carried in the tea-things. Deborah appeared shortly afterwards wearing a severe gown of dull gold velvet. Hannah noticed to her surprise that Lady Deborah, out of her masculine attire, was a very beautiful young woman.

'How,' said Deborah, pushing the wolfhound off the sofa and sitting down, 'can any civilized man watch a prize-fight?'

'When Benjamin won, you were cheering and I shouting fit to beat the band,' pointed out William.

Pym was cheering and shouting with relief. 'I thought the man would have been killed by Randall. But what an unusual cove of a footman you do have, Miss,'

Hannah reflected that it was a pity the beautiful Lady Deborah chose to speak in the words and accent of one of her grooms, before replying, 'Yes, he is very unusual. I do hope he has not decided to take up fighting as a career. Lord William, surely it was wrong of you to allow your sister to attend such an affair and expose her to ridicule.'

'They would have taken me for a man,' said Deborah hotly, 'had not Ashton put those about him wise.' Hannah's eyes fell on the roundness of Deborah's excellent bosom. 'I take leave to differ, my lady,' she said. 'You are very much a woman in appearance.'

William grinned. 'There you are, sis. Hear the lady speak. May as well resign yourself to a Season.'

'Never!' said Deborah passionately.

Thoroughly curious now, Hannah said, 'But may I point out, Lady Deborah, that at your age and with your beauty, I would expect you to be dreaming of beaux and balls.'

'I never wanted to be a woman,' said Deborah restlessly. 'They don't have no fun, nohow. All primping and simpering and laced into tight corsets and all so that they may catch the eye of some future husband. Pah! Husband? Slave-master, most like. Condemned to a life of breeding brats like a demned rabbit.'

Hannah chewed a caraway cake and eyed Deborah speculatively. Then she said, 'As

34

plain talking seems to be the order of the day, may I point out that your future seems to me singularly lonely and unpleasant.'

'How so?' Deborah, forgetting she was wearing skirts, swung one leg over the end of the sofa.

'When Lord William marries, his lady may not share your views on her sex; in fact, she might be very shocked. And if Lord William sets up his own establishment, who will you enjoy your freedom with? Surely the men of the county will not wish to hunt and fish and run wild with you? You will be damned as an Original, despised by both sexes.'

'William will never marry,' laughed Deborah. 'Can you see William in the toils of some pretty miss?'

'Oh, yes,' said Hannah quietly. 'Very easily.'

Deborah shifted restlessly. 'Here we are indoors on a fine day. Let's do something. What say, William? How can we amuse ourselves and Miss Pym until it is time to return her to Rochester?'

'Croquet,' exclaimed William. 'Just the thing for Miss Pym. Do you play, Miss Pym?'

'Yes, I do,' said Hannah. Mrs Clarence, wife of her late employer, had taught the servants to play one sunny day. Hannah could see her now, pretty little Mrs Clarence, her auburn hair glinting in the sunlight and her white muslin gown trailing across the green grass of the croquet lawn at Thornton Hall. And where

35

was Mrs Clarence now; Mrs Clarence who had run off with that footman and left her dour and depressed husband to end the rest of his days in morose solitude?

She wrenched her thoughts back to the present and soon she was out on the lawn at the front of the abbey with the twins. They played several light-hearted games, until the sun began to slant through the tall cypress trees at the edge of the grass.

They were just returning indoors when a carriage came rolling up the drive. The twins exchanged looks of dismay. 'Ashton!' they said in unison.

'Shall we tell Silvers not to admit him?' suggested William.

Deborah shrugged. 'Better not. He'll complain to Papa, and Papa was most odd when he was last home, worrying and fretting about us.'

'Shall I leave?' asked Hannah.

'No, do stay,' said Deborah. 'He can't bluster and rant with you present.'

They returned to the drawing-room, and shortly after they had settled themselves, the Earl of Ashton was announced.

Hannah studied him curiously. At first glance, she would have taken him for a dangerous rake, with his glittering green eyes and midnight-black hair and those odd slanting eyebrows, but responsibilities, not dissipation, she decided, had stamped those lines on either side of his mouth.

He declined any refreshment, shook hands with Hannah, and then sat down after tipping the contents of a chair onto the floor. 'Now,' he said, regarding the twins, 'I received a letter from your father asking me to look in on you and see you were not misbehaving yourselves.' He was, Hannah thought, very much the older man wearily preparing himself to lecture a couple of wayward schoolchildren. 'As you both will be able to understand, I was appalled to see Lady Deborah at a prize-fight and unsuitably dressed.'

'You are not our father, nor yet our guardian,' snapped Lady Deborah. 'What is it to you?'

'I am a friend of your father, as you both well know. Were it not for that, I would gladly leave you, Lady Deborah, to become the joke of the county.' Deborah flushed angrily. 'I shall keep a constant check on your behaviour, and if there is any repeat of anything like today's affair, I shall contact your father through our embassy in Constantinople and tell him to return.'

'You would not do that!' cried William.

'Oh, yes, I would. Now, I do not want to sit here lecturing both of you further. I have said what I came to say.' He turned to Hannah and said with a surprisingly charming smile, 'You made a gallant attempt to rescue your footman.'

'Benjamin is a silly boy,' said Hannah. 'I only pray he will not be marked for life.'

'I am curious,' said the earl. 'Where did you find such a servant?'

Hannah sat back and told him how she had found Benjamin and of all his adventures. The sun sank lower and the twins forgot their own troubles and listened with all the rapt fascinated interest of children hearing a bedtime story.

'You are lucky,' sighed Deborah when she had finished. 'Nothing exciting like that ever happens to us, does it, William?'

Before her brother could reply, Hannah said, 'Many would think being an object of ridicule was adventure enough, Lady Deborah.'

Deborah flushed and bit her lip. 'In fact,' pursued Hannah, 'you look so very charming in women's clothes, I am amazed you should ever choose to wear anything else.' She turned to the earl and said severely, 'As well as condemning Lady Deborah for attending such a spectacle, I find it strange that any civilized gentleman should choose to visit such an affair.'

'You have the right of it,' said the earl mildly. 'It had been years since I went to one, and believe me, it will be a long time before I will ever think of attending another. My tastes are dull and quiet, Miss Pym, and do not run to seeing two men beat each other to death.'

'I think you are interested in nothing else

but moralizing,' said Lady Deborah. 'You always were a dull stick, Ashton.'

Hannah stared at Deborah and raised her eyebrows. Deborah found herself blushing and added hotly, 'Why should I not do as I please? I ride and hunt and shoot better than any man I know.'

'Then you have only met milksops,' commented the earl acidly.

'My mare, Harriet, could outrun anything in your stables,' said Deborah.

He looked at her for a long moment and then said, 'I think you need to be taught a lesson, Lady Deborah. I shall race you, on the morrow.'

Deborah clapped her hands with glee. 'Where?'

'The drive of this abbey, from the lodge to the house. Two miles, is it not?'

'And what is the wager?' demanded Deborah.

He eyed her thoughtfully. 'If you win, I will leave you alone and interfere no more in your lives. Agreed?'

'Splendid,' said Deborah. 'And if I lose. . . although that will not happen.'

There was a long silence and then his voice fell on their ears, light and amused, 'If you lose, Lady Deborah, then you will give me a kiss.'

'Here, I say,' protested William, 'what kind of wager is that?'

The earl looked at Deborah, his eyes alight with mockery. 'Frightened?' he asked softly.

Deborah tossed her head. 'Not I.' She held out a small hand. The earl took it and shook it solemnly. 'Shall we say eleven o'clock tomorrow morning? And who is to be judge?'

William crowed with laughter. 'Why, the excellent Miss Pym, o' course. Those sharp eyes of hers will act as judge and jury. Hey, what say you, Miss Pym?'

'I should be delighted,' said Hannah, her eyes gleaming almost as green as the earl's as they looked from Lady Deborah's flushed face to the earl's mocking one.

'Then I shall take my leave.' The earl swept them a low bow and left the room.

'I hope you know what you're about, Deb,' said William. 'He seems pretty confident.'

'Pooh!' said Deborah. 'I shall win, never fear. Now let us get Miss Pym back to that inn of hers.'

By the time they arrived at the Crown, Hannah had decided that Deborah and William were a very good-hearted couple. It was a pity they had been allowed to run wild. They treated her with a casual friendliness, as if they had known her a very long time. She invited them to supper and they cheerfully agreed. They all sat down round the long inn table. Captain Beltravers was there and Mrs Conningham and her daughter and the three had heard all about the prize-fight but wanted Hannah's description of it. As Hannah talked, she watched Miss Abigail Conningham's expressive face. The girl did not look quite so plain now. Her eyes, although still rather small, were not puffy anymore and her mousy brown hair had been dressed in quite a pretty style. While she talked, Hannah wondered what it was about going to stay with Uncle in Dover that was so upsetting Miss Conningham. When she had finished, Captain Beltravers said, 'I heard your footman has been carried off in triumph to London.'

Hannah's heart sank. She would miss Benjamin. She thought sadly that he might have waited just to say goodbye. He was not much use at household chores, but as a bodyguard he was excellent. She would miss his outrageous remarks and clever face.

'From what you have already told us,' she realized Lady Deborah was saying, 'you appear to enjoy journeying on the stage. Why is that, Miss Pym?'

Hannah told them of her legacy, but not that she had been a servant, for Lady Deborah might shrink from her, and Hannah was anxious to see the outcome of the race in the morning. 'I had led a very quiet life,' said Hannah, thinking briefly of the dark, dreary days when Mr Clarence had shut up half of Thornton Hall where she had been housekeeper and when the parties and dinners

41

and entertainments had ceased. 'I used to watch the Flying Machines going along the Kensington road,' said Hannah. 'All that colour and movement flashing by. And I have had such adventures since I began my travels this year.'

'I wish I could have adventures,' sighed Deborah.

The captain smiled at her and said gently, 'Some would say attending a prize-fight dressed in masculine attire was an adventure, Lady Deborah.'

'I made a mistake,' said Deborah repressively. 'I am sorry you heard of it. My escapade is obviously the talk of Rochester.'

'Do you wear men's clothes because you wish you were a man?' asked Abigail and then coloured at her own temerity.

'Not quite,' said Deborah. 'But I envy men their freedom.'

'Men sometimes envy women,' said the captain. 'They do not have to fight wars, they do not have to worry about providing for a family, they are never subjected to danger.'

'But men can choose whom they marry,' said Abigail. 'They are not constrained to marry someone they don't know, and what is more, don't want to!' And with that, she burst into tears and ran from the table, with her scandalized mother hurrying after her.

There was a startled silence after she had left, and then Hannah said slowly, 'Ah,

I think that explains the mystery of Miss Conningham's distress. At Dover, there is some suitor that has been picked out for her.'

The door of the dining-room opened and Benjamin walked in. He went straight up to Hannah and stood behind her chair.

Hannah's eyes filled with tears of sheer gladness. 'I think we would like another bottle of claret, Benjamin.'

'Very good, modom,' said Benjamin and went to fetch the waiter.

Hannah very much wanted the return of Benjamin to pass over quietly, but Deborah and her brother were wildly excited and plied Benjamin with questions when he returned with the wine. Had he feared for his life? Was he badly hurt? Benjamin was wearing blanc to cover his bruises, and his hair had been freshly powdered. He replied quietly to all their questions until Hannah, shooting an anxious look up at him, realized he was exhausted and ordered him to bed.

The party broke up, Deborah and William cheerfully asking Captain Beltravers to come and see the race. 'And bring poor little Miss Conningham with you,' called Deborah over her shoulder as she reached the inn door. The captain flushed slightly and said he would certainly see if she wanted to go. Hannah Pym noticed that tell-tale flush and her mind worked busily. Here was a fine upstanding captain and a young girl who obviously did not want to marry her family's, or perhaps her uncle's choice. She did not for a moment consider the possibility of a romance between the Earl of Ashton and Lady Deborah Western.

They were poles apart!

3

There is always one who kisses and one who only allows the kiss.

George Bernard Shaw

Miss Abigail Conningham seemed to have put her troubles aside for the day, as a party consisting of herself, her mother, the captain, Hannah and Benjamin set out from the inn on the following morning to travel to Downs Abbey.

The hedges were starred with bird cherry and a pale sun glittered on the incredible green of the new leaves. Benjamin had hired a cabriolet with two sturdy horses and was obviously enjoying acting the part of coachman as they bowled along the leafy lanes where blackbirds and thrushes sang from the high hedges on either side.

Miss Conningham, Hannah noticed, had embellished the shoulders of her plain brown gown with knots of tartan ribbon. Hannah, seated next to Mrs Conningham, decided to enliven the shortjourney by finding out exactly why the lady and her daughter were travelling to Dover. To her first question, Mrs Conningham replied briefly that they were to visit Abigail's Uncle Henry, her own brother-in-law, a wealthy merchant.

'Your daughter does not appear to be looking forward to the visit,' said Hannah.

'She will come about when she gets there,' said Mrs Conningham. 'Young girls have their heads stuffed full of romantic notions. She must do as she is bid.'

'That being?' asked Hannah, whose curiosity was mounting by leaps and bounds.

Mrs Conningham looked at her a trifle impatiently and then said reluctantly in a low voice, 'Uncle Henry, Mr Bentley, that is, has come most timely to my aid. My husband died two years since and we are in straitened circumstances. He wrote to say he had found a husband for Abigail and sent his miniature. A most worthy man by the name of Josiah Clegg, a widower, a trifle old, in his forties, but just the sort of steady influence a girl like Abigail needs.'

'Rich?'

'Very.'

'Ah.' Hannah sat back and folded her hands on the silver top of her umbrella. Mystery solved. She glanced at the captain, who was pointing out a ruined tower to Abigail. The normally harsh lines of his face were softer that morning. Definitely early thirties, Hannah decided. Old enough, but not so old as this Mr Clegg.

She returned to the topic. 'And why does Miss Conningham not favour this Mr Clegg? Does she consider him too old? Or did she take against his miniature?'

'Both,' said Abigail's mother succinctly. 'She said he looked like a fox.'

'And does he?' pursued Hannah. 'Look like a fox, I mean?'

'Miss Pym,' said Mrs Conningham severely, 'I do not want to spoil this pleasant outing by pulling caps, but I must take leave to tell you that your questions are beginning to border on the impertinent.'

'I beg your pardon,' said Hannah earnestly. 'Let us talk about something else. I confess I am looking forward to this race.'

Mrs Conningham gave an indulgent laugh. 'Fancy a beautiful lady such as Lady Deborah challenging a gentleman to a horse-race!' Hannah smiled, but thought privately that Mrs Conningham would not be nearly so tolerant if the race were to be ridden by some tavern wench. Obviously Lady Deborah's rank forgave a lot.

The party arrived at the abbey and were ushered inside and offered spiced ale, 'to prime them for the great event', as Lord William put it. Flags had been put up outside

46

the front door of the abbey to mark the finishing line. Hannah was to stand there and decide the winner. The captain and Lord William were to position themselves at the lodge gates to start the race off. Lady Deborah was wearing a man's riding-dress with a colourful belcher handkerchief knotted around her throat and a low-crowned wide-brimmed hat on her head. Hannah privately thought she made a dashing figure but Mrs Conningham was very shocked. She had expected Lady Deborah to ride side-saddle. Everyone knew, after all, that riding astride could ruin a young miss's virginity.

The inn party had arrived early, and so they had at least half an hour to await the arrival of the earl. Hannah took a seat next to Captain Beltravers.

'Why are you travelling to Dover?' she asked.

'To rejoin my regiment, ma'am,' he said.

'Have you a wife waiting for you?'

His face darkened. 'Not any longer. She died.'

'I am so sorry, so very sorry,' said Hannah. 'What happened?'

'I had a good wife, Mary, and a baby boy,' he said heavily. 'Mary was overjoyed to get a "to-go" ticket when I was posted to the Low Countries. I was delighted as well. We would be together. Had I known what it would be like, I would never have let my wife and boy

47

come. Often they had to sleep out in the hard frost with me with only a thin blanket to cover us. Once I found she was missing when we were on the march and went back to look for her. She was sitting exhausted by the roadside with the baby in her arms and all the laundry, still wet from the washing, and the household goods on her back. Not long after that, disaster struck. I had got her a donkey and she and the child were fording a river when the donkey slipped and threw them both into the icy water. I plunged in and swam downstream after them, but by the time I got them out, both were dead. I went on soldiering. It is all I know. To be frank, ma'am, these long days I do not care much what I do.'

Hannah pressed his hand sympathetically, tears in her eyes. She forgot about trying to make a match between the captain and Abigail. After such a dreadful loss, the captain would probably never entertain any romantic thoughts toward a female again.

She felt very low in spirits and was relieved when the Earl of Ashton was announced. He was accompanied by Mr Peter Carruthers and a young lady who turned out to be Mr Carruthers's sister, Clarissa. Clarissa was all giggles and bouncing curls and large brown eyes. Deborah flicked her a glance of contempt and then was mortified to see that her brother, William, appeared to be highly entertained by Clarissa.

48

Deborah's spirits were further lowered by the slightly amazed looks Clarissa kept throwing in her direction and by the open contempt with which Mr Carruthers viewed her male attire.

'You can still change your mind,' mocked the earl.

Deborah flushed angrily. 'And so may you, sir. I have no fear. I will beat you fair and square.'

'We will see,' he said, his green eyes glinting. Clarissa came up to him and handed him a little lace handkerchief. 'What is this?' he asked, looking indulgently down at her.

'My favour,' said Clarissa with a trill of laughter. 'Like the knights of old. You must put it in your hat.'

'Gladly,' he said, taking it from her.

'Yes, you will need all the help you can get,' commented Deborah waspishly. Clarissa looked at her in round-eyed fright and edged behind the earl for protection, rather like a child going behind its mother's skirts.

William joined them and held out his arm to Clarissa. 'Will you do me the honour of coming with me to start the race?'

Clarissa smiled up at him, eyes dancing, curls bobbing, and gave a little skip. 'I should like that above all things,' she said.

The earl regarded the couple thoughtfully as they moved off, talking animatedly. He turned back to Deborah. 'Most suitable,' he remarked.

'What is?' she demanded angrily, although she knew very well what he meant.

'Why, Miss Carruthers and Lord William, to be sure. I would say they were eminently suited.'

Deborah was outraged to hear her fears put into words. 'William and that silly little miss!' she sputtered. 'He prefers the company of his sister above all other females, let me tell you.'

'He cannot fall in love with his sister,' said the earl acidly, his eyes raking up and down her riding-dress. 'Nor will any man fall in love with you, Lady Deborah, if you persist in looking like a boy.'

Deborah went quite white with anger. 'You are trying to put me in a passion so that I may ride badly and lose the race.'

'Not I,' said the earl lazily. 'As a good friend of your father, my remarks were prompted by concern for your future, that is all. Are you ready?'

'I am ready,' said Deborah in a thin voice. Outside, he studied her mare, Harriet, with an appraising eye. 'Fine beast,' he said.

'And she goes like the wind,' crowed Deborah.

Her eyes fell on the earl's horse, which a groom was just bringing up, and she felt a pang of unease. It was a coal-black stallion, an Arab, with a small proud head.

They both mounted and cantered easily

down the long drive to the lodge gates.

William and Clarissa were already there and so were the captain and Abigail, William having driven them all in an open carriage to the start of the race.

Hannah and Mr Carruthers, surrounded by the abbey servants, took up their position at the finishing line, which was marked by frivolous lilac silk ribbon tied between two flags.

She did so hope Lady Deborah would lose. She was a fine good-hearted girl but needed to be taught a lesson. 'But why?' thought Hannah, suddenly and rebelliously. In this age when women were confined by modes and manners as tight as their stays, it was refreshing to meet a young miss who rose free of them all. But that freedom would lead to spinsterhood and a childless existence, and Hannah, who suffered from both these curses, did not want any other female to bear them. In her few darker moments, Hannah often dreamt of the children she would like to have had. She was joined by Mrs Conningham who remarked acridly that she would be glad when this nonsense was over. 'Is Miss Conningham your only child?' asked Hannah.

'I have eight others,' said Mrs Conningham repressively, 'and so you see, it is important that Abigail marries well.'

How unromantic this business of marriage was, thought Hannah with a sigh.

Down at the end of the drive, the riders were ready. Deborah's blue eyes were flashing with excitement. She was so sure of winning that she had lost all nervousness. Had she not outridden every man in the county on the hunting field?

William, with Clarissa beside him, held up a large handkerchief. 'Ready?' he called, and both riders nodded. He brought the large handkerchief down with a great sweep. Clarissa squealed with excitement and the earl and Deborah set off like the wind. At first they were neck and neck and then, to Deborah's horror, with almost contemptuous ease, the earl spurred his horse and began to move ahead of her, almost as if he had been previously holding his great horse in check.

His horse surged forward, black muscles rippling along its flanks.

Hannah watched the earl come thundering up. His horse broke through the lightly tied ribbon, swept round in front of the abbey and then he reined it in and came riding slowly back. Deborah, who, seeing that the race was lost, had slowed her mount, was at the finishing line, her face tight and set.

'A good race, my lord,' she called. 'What a magnificent beast.'

He swung himself lightly down from the saddle and walked over to her and put a hand on her stirrup and looked up at her. 'I claim my bet,' he said.

'A bet!' cried Mr Carruthers. 'Have you lost much money, Lady Deborah?'

'Only a kiss,' said the earl lightly.

William and his party came driving up, William looking sympathetically at his sister's set face. 'If you're going to claim your bet, Ashton,' called William to the earl, who had walked a few steps away to talk to Mr Carruthers, 'I suggest you take Deb into the house. Servants watching, don't you know.'

Deborah dismounted. The earl came back to her and held out his arm. She took it gingerly and he led her toward the house.

'Hope she throws everything in the room at his head,' said William.

* * *

The earl stood with Deborah in the hall. He put his hands lightly on her shoulders. 'Afraid?' he asked softly.

'Not I,' said Deborah, throwing back her head. 'Get on with it.'

He bent his head to place a fleeting kiss on her mouth. But as soon as his lips touched hers, he felt just as if he had received an electric shock from one of Dr Galvani's machines. He buried his lips deeper in hers and wrapped his arms tightly about her. His long fingers buried themselves in her shining curls. And Deborah stood unresisting in his arms, unable to do anything other than return his kiss.

He finally raised his head and looked down at her. 'Well,' he said shakily. 'Well . . .'

Deborah backed slowly away from him, one hand to her mouth, her eyes wide and blank. 'I must change,' she said huskily and ran from him up the wide staircase, her spurs jingling. He stood in the hall, shaking his head slowly as though to clear it. Then he remembered the others were waiting tactfully outside and went to tell them the wager had been claimed.

William, who would normally have been worried about his sister, was too taken up with the charms of Miss Carruthers and too depressed at her news that she was returning to London in the morning. 'Where are you staying?' asked William.

'With the Chumleys on the other side of Rochester.'

'And in London?'

'With my parents in Green Street.'

William took a deep breath. 'I shall be going to London shortly,' he said. 'May I call on you?'

Clarissa lowered her long eyelashes. 'Yes, please do,' she whispered.

William felt almost sick with elation. He led her with the others to the dining-room, where a cold collation had been laid out for the guests.

He sat down next to Clarissa and helped her

to food as tenderly as if she were an invalid. He dimly heard Hannah asking where Lady Deborah was and he did not care.

'Lady Deborah has gone to change,' said the earl. Mr Carruthers leaned forward and said to Hannah, 'I am sure we have met before. Is that possible?'

'No, I do not think so, sir.' Hannah looked at him uneasily.

'Odd, and yet I know I have seen you somewhere before, ma'am. It is those remarkable eyes of yours. Let me think.'

Hannah prayed that Lady Deborah would come in and create a diversion. When Mrs Clarence had been in residence at Thornton Hall, there had been many parties and many guests. If Mr Carruthers had been one of them and remembered her as the housekeeper and said so, she feared all would shrink from her.

The door opened and Lady Deborah came in. She was wearing a pretty gown of lilac jaconet muslin with a gored bodice finished with a tucker of fine embroidery. The gentlemen rose to their feet. Lady Deborah looked around the table rather blindly, but the only vacant seat was next to the earl and he was drawing out the chair for her. She sat down, her back ramrod-straight, and stared straight ahead.

'I know where I have seen you before,' cried Mr Carruthers suddenly. The earl noticed that Miss Pym's strange footman, who was standing

55

behind her chair, put a hand on his mistress's shoulder and gripped it hard. Hannah's eyes were quite colourless.

'It was in Gunter's,' cried Mr Carruthers. 'And you were taking tea with Sir George Clarence.'

'Yes, Sir George is a friend of mine,' said Hannah, her eyes golden. The footman, the earl noticed, removed his hand from Hannah's shoulder and visibly appeared to relax.

The earl turned his attention to Deborah. She looked up at him. How blue her eyes were, he thought, as blue as the summer sea. He was intensely aware of her now, of the rise and fall of her soft bosom, of those excellent slender legs now decorously concealed beneath a skirt, of the springy curl of her golden hair, which framed her face like an aureole.

'How do you and your brother pass your days, Lady Deborah?' he asked.

'In various sports,' she answered, 'and in seeing to the smooth running of the estate.'

'Do you make calls?'

'No, only on sick tenants. I despise this business of making calls, chattering inanely among the teacups.'

'Ah, I had forgot, you despise your own sex.'

'I do not despise ladies such as Miss Pym, for example, who have wind and bottom, but flirting, empty-headed misses, that is another thing.' She looked sourly in the direction of Clarissa, who was trilling with laughter at something her brother had said. William appeared enchanted.

'I am glad to notice that Lord William does not share your views,' said the earl drily.

'Everything was all right before you came,' muttered Deborah, and stabbed a piece of meat viciously with her two-pronged fork.

Hannah, quite light-headed with relief that Mr Carruthers had not found out her guilty secret, began to regale the company with some of her adventures. 'Tell them about Benjamin,' urged William, and so Hannah told them about the wicked Lady Carsey and how Benjamin had found employment in her household. He had learned she had a penchant for what she deemed as freaks, although most would deem as unfortunate, and so had pretended to be deaf and dumb, how he had been rescued from the scaffold and of how Lady Carsey had tried to take her revenge by subsequently kidnapping him, a rescue only achieved after Hannah had set Lady Carsey's house on fire.

'A dangerous woman,' said Mr Carruthers. 'Be careful she does not cross your path again, Miss Pym.'

'I shall be very careful,' said Hannah. 'Up until I met her, I thought there was a spark of good in all of us, but I think Lady Carsey is evil.'

'And so your Benjamin, instead of going ahead to be one of England's greatest fighters, decided out of gratitude to stay as your servant,' said Mr Carruthers.

''Ere!' said Benjamin, finding his voice. 'I stay 'cos I wants to stay. What's the fun o' getting smashed in the victualling-box?'

There was a roar of laughter at this from all except Clarissa, who looked at Hannah in round-eyed amazement. 'I fear we are shocking Miss Clarissa,' said William.

'I could never do such things,' said Clarissa. 'I should be frightened to death.' She shrank a little toward William, who laughed and patted her hand and called her a silly puss.

Deborah looked crossly at William and reflected that she had never seen her brother make such a cake of himself before.

She was glad when the meal was over and prayed these unwelcome guests would soon take themselves off, but there was William, offering to take Clarissa on a tour of the gardens. 'Well, Lady Deborah,' mocked the earl, 'are the rest of us to be neglected? Or may we see the gardens?'

'If you wish,' said Deborah crossly. The company all rinsed out their mouths and wiped them on the tablecloth, napkins still being considered a newfangled French custom. Deborah led the way out.

The day was warm and balmy. She walked quickly to try to keep up with her brother and Clarissa, who were heading for the rose garden. She had a sudden stabbing fear that

William would do something insane like propose marriage.

'Not so fast,' she heard the earl say. 'It is too fine a day to charge along. Besides, your brother is old enough to look after himself.'

'He may do something he might regret,' snapped Deborah. 'Imagine having that as a sister-in-law.'

'You could fare worse,' he said easily. 'She is sweet and kind.'

'Pooh,' exclaimed Deborah. 'She would bore him to death!'

He caught her arm and swung her round to face him. 'Perhaps not. There is such a thing as love.'

Her eyes flew up to meet his and then dropped. She tugged her arm away and said, 'You only say such things to torment me.'

'Not I. As I pointed out earlier, I have your welfare at heart.'

'Why?'

'Because of my friendship with your father.'

'Of course. You are old, like my father, are you not?'

He studied her flushed face. 'Not a worthy remark,' he said. 'Let us walk on.' Deborah marched beside him. 'Here we are at the rose garden,' he said, 'and there are your brother and Miss Carruthers, standing by the sundial, looking very romantic.'

'Fiddle. The roses are not yet out. There is nothing to see but thorns and leaves.'

'Which is exactly what I think when I look at you,' said the earl.

Deborah made an impatient noise and went to join her brother, but for the first time William looked as if he heartily wished her elsewhere.

'I see Captain Beltravers has walked off with your daughter,' Hannah was saying to Mrs Conningham. 'Are you not concerned?'

'No,' said Mrs Conningham placidly. 'The captain is a gentleman and I felt it my duty to tell him during luncheon that Abigail was already engaged. Let us sit down, Miss Pym. The day is quite warm.'

Both ladies sat down on a rustic bench. Hannah watched the retreating figures of Abigail and Captain Beltravers and wondered what the normally silent and withdrawn soldier was finding to talk about.

'Uncle Henry is very wealthy,' Abigail was saying sadly. 'He could have provided for the lot of us, that is, Mother and all my brothers and sisters, and barely have noticed the difference. Oh, he has said now, he will help, but only if I marry this Mr Clegg.'

'It is a miserable situation for you,' commented the captain. 'Can nothing be done?'

Abigail shook her head. 'I am twenty and Mama says I will soon be on the shelf. My sister Jane is nineteen and the beauty of the family. She told me I was being a ninny and that I would have a grand house and all the clothes I wanted.'

'Then why did not Jane take your place?'

'Because Mama says the eldest must be married first and that Jane with her looks can find a husband anywhere.'

'Perhaps when you are in Dover, you can appeal to your uncle's good nature.'

'As I recall,' said Abigail, 'he hasn't got a good nature.'

He walked along beside her in silence for quite a while and then said, 'I have been thinking of Miss Pym and her adventures, Miss Conningham. She seems a very competent and strong lady. Might it not be an idea to talk to her? I cannot think of any solution, but she may.'

Abigail brightened and turned to him. 'Do you think so? Do you really think so?'

'Anything is better than being without hope,' he replied in a low voice.

'Oh,' said Abigail with quick sympathy. 'I heard you telling Miss Pym about your wife and child. How very terrible for you and how you must hate the military and everything to do with it.'

He looked at her in surprise. 'I never thought about it,' he said slowly. 'I have always been a soldier.'

'But don't you see,' cried Abigail, looking almost pretty in her concern for him, 'everything must remind you of your sad loss.

When you go on campaigns, and see other wives being treated badly, it all must remind you of your lost wife. If I were you, I would hate my superior officers for being such callous monsters.'

She stopped and turned to face him, tears standing out in her eyes and her face flushed.

'Why, Miss Abigail,' exclaimed the captain. 'I . . . I . . . well, by George, you have the right of it.'

'But can you afford to sell out?' asked Abigail delicately.

'Yes, yes,' he said impatiently. 'That is the tragedy, don't you see? If my Mary had stayed at home, she could have lived in comfort. There was no need for her to come. But I was heedless and thoughtless. I tell you, Miss Abigail, I sometimes look on myself as a murderer.'

He suddenly sat down on the grass and began to cry.

Abigail sank down beside him, her skirts spreading out over the grass. 'There now,' she said helplessly. 'There! It is all over, and Mary and your boy are in Heaven and looking down on you. They are with the angels and very happy, that I do know.' She put an arm about his shaking shoulders and held him until the spasm of grief had passed. He scrubbed his eyes and said half-ashamed, 'I should not have inflicted my grief on you.'

'You had to cry sometime,' said Abigail

practically. 'I do believe, Captain Beltravers, that this is the first time you have ever cried.'

He nodded dumbly. 'Then we will rise and continue our walk,' said Abigail in a motherly voice, 'until you have recovered yourself, and then we will return to the abbey and find you a fortifying glass of brandy.'

He rose and helped her to her feet, holding both of her hands tightly. 'I shall never forget you,' he said quietly and then dropped her hands as if suddenly embarrassed. Abigail blushed and then tucked her hand in his arm and together they walked off across the lawns.

Hannah, discussing the best ways of whitening linen with Mrs Conningham, covertly watched the two tiny figures disappear from view. She wondered if the captain had any money. She wondered why Lady Deborah looked changed since that kiss which must have taken place. She wondered about all sorts of interesting things while a small part of her mind coped with the domestic conversation with Mrs Conningham.

At last, she saw Lady Deborah returning from the rose garden. She was alone and looked in a furious temper. Behind her came William, stooping down to hear what the dainty little Clarissa was saying, and behind them strolled the earl with his friend, Mr Carruthers.

Then from the other direction came Abigail

with the captain, no longer a shy Abigail but a determined lady who asked if the captain might have some brandy because he had been feeling unwell.

They all went up to the drawing-room, where the captain was given a bumper of brandy by William. The rest were served with wine and cakes. Hannah noticed that despite the masculine chaos that usually reigned in the rooms of the abbey, the house boasted an excellent cook and the twins were good hosts. Some effort had been made to clean up the jumble which normally filled the drawing-room and the dogs were mercifully absent.

Mrs Conningham, aware that her daughter was fussing too much around the captain, announced loudly that they should take their leave. Mr Carruthers said he and his sister had to make arrangements for their journey to London in the morning. Benjamin left to bring the carriage round.

On the journey back to the inn, Captain Beltravers set himself to talk to Mrs Conningham and kept that lady so interested that Hannah was able to turn the events of the day over in her mind in peace. They were to leave Rochester on the repaired stage-coach in the morning. That, thought Hannah, was a pity, for she had become interested in Lord William and Lady Deborah. She would have liked to know whether Lady Deborah thought of the earl at all and what she thought and if William meant seriously to court Clarissa.

*　　*　　*

There was a long silence in the drawing-room after the guests had left. The dogs were allowed back in. William put his booted feet on the table and yawned and then said, 'Dashed fine girl.'

'The Clarissa creature? Pooh! You don't half make a cake of yourself when you set your mind to it,' sneered his sister.

He grinned. 'I would call losing a race and having to kiss the winner making a cake of m'self. How was it, Deb? I'll bet our Puritan Ashley gave you a chaste kiss on the brow.'

'Something like that,' said Deborah quickly. 'Don't let's talk about him. Were you really taken with that simpering, chattering fool?'

William eyed her levelly. 'Don't ever, not ever, speak of Clarissa Carruthers in such terms again. Do I make myself clear?'

Deborah looked at him in dismay. 'But I was funning. You really did fancy her?'

'Yes,' said William quietly. 'And next week I plan to go to London to stay with Aunt Jill so's I can call on Miss Carruthers.'

'If you marry, William, where would you live?'

'Why, here,' said William, looking around. 'Bags of room.'

'Oh.' Deborah pleated the skirt of her gown with nervous fingers. Everything was changing so quickly. And there was not much to divert William. The hunting season was over. She could not let him sit and brood about this Clarissa or he would rush off to London and propose to her on the spot and then Clarissa would be the lady of Downs Abbey, prattling about the rooms, boring the very air with her inane remarks. She must think up something to amuse her brother so that he would forget the existence of Miss Carruthers.

'I like that Miss Pym,' said Deborah. 'What a character. I swear that adventures must follow her around. I like hearing her stories. Curst flat here, ain't it?'

'You'd best stop talking like that, Deb,' said William severely. 'Won't do for a lady's drawing-room.'

'Oh, as you will,' said Deborah hurriedly. 'Tell you what, we've never travelled on the stage. Why don't we pack bags and go down to the Crown and have supper, stay the night and take the stage to Dover in the morning?'

William looked doubtful. 'You can't really call on your Clarissa until next week,' pursued Deborah. 'I mean you'll need to warn Aunt Jill of your arrival.'

His face cleared. 'Capital idea, but just one thing.'

'What?'

'Dress like a woman, would you?'

66

Deborah was about to shout at him that she would dress any way she pleased, but that might mean he would not go and William must be diverted at all costs, lest the terrible Clarissa would soon be in residence.

*   *   *

The Earl of Ashton felt strangely depressed. Usually he was perfectly happy in the evenings with his own company. He found he had a desire to ride back to Downs Abbey but could not think up a logical reason for doing so. He remembered a neighbour, Sir Paul Langford, had house guests and that he had promised he might, just might, call in later, although he had refused an invitation to supper. There would be company, for the Langfords liked to entertain, and noise and music.

On impulse, he ordered his carriage and told his valet to lay out his evening clothes. Soon he was changed and travelling on his way to the Langfords'.

Sir Paul had a comfortable mansion which was lit from top to bottom when the earl arrived. He hesitated for a moment, suddenly regretting his impulse, but the grooms were already holding his horses' heads and the butler was standing on the steps to receive him. He could hardly turn about and drive off.

Supper was over and the company were assembled in the music room listening to a lady carolling popular ballads.

He smiled across at Sir Paul and took a chair at the back of the room.

He became aware that a lady close by was studying him. He glanced at her. She caught his eye and smiled slowly, a seductive smile, and he felt his senses quicken. She was of mature years, but quite striking with her large eyes and oiled brown hair dressed in one of the latest Roman fashions. She had an excellent white bosom, most of which was bared, showing half of each nipple, which had been rouged. He wondered who she was and then thought this saucy lady who was throwing him such inviting glances might be the very thing to take the taste of that bewitching kiss from Lady Deborah out of his mouth and out of his mind.

When the concert was over, the guests started to stroll about the rooms. Sir Paul came up to him, and at the same time, there was the lady of the rouged nipples, fanning herself slowly and obviously waiting for an introduction.

'May I present the Earl of Ashton. . . Lady Carsey,' said Sir Paul.

Now where, thought the earl, have I heard that name before?

He bowed over her hand. 'Did you go to the prize-fight, Ashton?' asked Sir Paul.

'Yes,' said the earl, 'but we must not discuss prize-fights in front of the ladies.'

'On the contrary,' said Lady Carsey. 'I believe it was quite an event. The famous Randall beaten by an unknown.'

'A strange fellow,' said Sir Paul with a laugh. 'Name of Benjamin Stubbs. Could have made himself a fortune as a fighter, but after he had won he returned like a lamb to his duties as footman to some spinster who is travelling on the stage to Rochester.'

Just as Lady Carsey went very still and her eyes sharpened, the earl realized where he had heard her name before. This then was the dangerous Lady Carsey who had nearly had Benjamin killed.

'They will all be in Dover by now, I think,' he said lightly. 'I mean, the fighter and his mistress.'

'Oh, no,' said Sir Paul jovially. 'Stage was up at Limmers' for repairs. Leaves in the morning.'

The earl bowed to Lady Carsey and then walked off, nodding to a few acquaintances before he was able to politely take his leave. He must warn Miss Pym that Benjamin's old tormentor was not only in the vicinity but knew of his whereabouts.

4

And almost every one when age,
Disease, or sorrows strike him,
Inclines to think there is a God,
Or something very like Him.
                    Arthur Hugh Clough

Hannah was polishing the furniture in her inn bedchamber as a way of relaxing before going down to supper when there came a knock at the door. She guiltily thrust the duster in her trunk, knowing that a visitor would think it strange in the extreme that any lady would perform a job that inn servants were paid to do—with the exception of Benjamin, who would nonetheless give her a lecture on what a lady should do and should not do.

She opened the door. Abigail Conningham stood there, looking at her nervously. 'May I beg a word in private with you, Miss Pym?'

Hannah nodded, her eyes gleaming green with curiosity. They sat in chairs on either side of the fireplace. 'Captain Beltravers suggested I should talk to you,' said Abigail earnestly to the corner of the mantelshelf.

'Ah!'

'You see, I am being taken to my uncle's in Dover so that I may wed a friend of his, a Mr Clegg.'

'So I have heard,' said Hannah, and waited for more.

'I have been very miserable about it—am miserable. But I comforted myself nonetheless by thinking I was doing my duty. Uncle Henry has promised to give Mama money for our upkeep if I wed Mr Clegg. But now we are so very nearly at Dover, I feel quite desperate. I confided as much to Captain Beltravers and he suggested I should talk to you about the matter.'

'Very proper.' Hannah folded her hands in her lap. 'First tell me: is your family in very straitened circumstances?'

'I believe so, although since Papa died, which was two years ago, Mama has handled the purse-strings. I have eight brothers and sisters, all younger than I. There is Jane, of course. She is nineteen and very beautiful and would not have minded in the slightest had Uncle Henry chosen her for Mr Clegg. She says she longs for an establishment of her own, for she has to share a bedchamber with me and that she does not like. I have tried to talk to Mama about this, but when I do, she cries and calls me selfish and ungrateful. I am sure I am, for many of my friends have married without a murmur those chosen for them by their parents.'

'It is kind of Captain Beltravers to interest himself in your predicament,' said Hannah. 'He is a fine man.'

'Oh, yes.' Abigail's eyes glowed. 'I pride myself that I was able to be of help to him.'

'How so?'

'He told you of the death of his wife and child?' Hannah nodded. 'So I was able to make him realize that he no longer likes being a soldier and should sell out.'

'He may not be able to,' said Hannah cautiously.

'The captain said he was not short of money.'

'Then why is he only a captain at his age?' demanded Hannah. 'In this perfidious age, the higher ranks are there for the buying.'

'I believe it takes influence as well as money,' said Abigail wisely. 'Oh, but much as I long to see the captain happy, I can really only think of myself. What am I to do?'

'I think,' said Hannah, 'that the best thing is for me to call on your uncle when we reach Dover and point out to him that you have a prettier and more willing younger sister. Would that answer?'

Abigail shook her head dismally. 'I have not seen him for four years or more, but I remember him as being choleric and made even more so if his will is crossed.'

'I will think of something,' said Hannah bracingly. 'I, Hannah Pym, do swear this. You will not have to marry Mr Clegg if I have any say in the matter. Now, I suggest you should keep as much as possible in the company of

72

Captain Beltravers. The company of a good man is always a useful education for a young girl. Leave it all to me.'

Abigail rose and shyly leaned over and kissed Hannah on the cheek. 'Thank you,' she said simply.

Benjamin came into the room just after Abigail had left. 'We have a difficult task, Benjamin,' said Hannah when they were alone. 'By the way, did you pay that gambling debt I heard you had incurred?'

'Of course, modom. What is this task?'

Hannah succinctly outlined Abigail's problem.

Benjamin sank into a chair and stretched out his long legs. Hannah frowned. Benjamin, like the good footman he ought to be, should never sit down in her presence, but as he was obviously thinking hard, she decided to ignore the social lapse.

'Why,' said Benjamin finally, 'if I were you, modom, I'd find out the address in London of Miss Abigail and send sister Jane money for the stage to Dover, saying as how she'd be a better wife for old Clegg. If she's as beautiful as all that, this Clegg should be delighted.'

'You are a genius,' cried Hannah. 'Get me pen and ink and paper. There is an up mail coach due any moment now and I can send it off.'

She busied herself writing, enclosed some paper money, sanded the letter, sealed it and handed it to Benjamin, who ran off with it to catch the mail. Hannah felt a glow of satisfaction. It seemed a long time since she had taken any decisive action.

Hannah went down to supper. The others were already there, Abigail looking suspiciously red about the eyes again and Mrs Conningham sitting between her daughter and the captain and occasionally darting sharp little looks at each.

Before the first course was served, Deborah and William arrived, cheerfully sure of a welcome, and sat down, Deborah saying they had decided it would be no end of a lark to go with the stage to Dover in the morning.

The idea of travelling in such exalted company took Mrs Conningham's mind away from the captain and her daughter. A loud cheer from outside the inn heralded the arrival of Benjamin. He was very much a hero in the town.

'What made you decide to go to Dover?' asked Hannah.

'We were bored,' replied William, 'and besides, I am sure if we stayed, Puritan Ashton would be round to give us a jaw-me-dead.'

'Lord Ashton did not appear a Puritan to me,' said Hannah. 'A Puritan would not encourage a young lady to match him in a horserace, nor would he kiss her.'

'That was just Ashton's irritating way of trying to teach Deb a lesson,' pointed out

William, and his sister glowered.

'Why! Here is the very gentleman,' said Hannah, looking across the dining-room to see the arrival of the earl. He was dauntingly resplendent in a single-breasted coat of black velvet with a ruffled shirt worn under a richly embroidered satin waistcoat. His knee breeches, also of black velvet, were fastened with gold buckles, as were his shoes, and he wore a dress sword, a large ruby gleaming on the hilt.

He sat down next to Hannah and refused any supper. 'I came here to warn you,' he said. Deborah looked disappointed. She had been sure he had come to see her again. 'Warn us about what?' asked William.

The earl sighed heavily. 'Not you. I did not even know you were here. It is to Miss Pym and her servant that I bring my warning. This evening, I visited friends, the Langfords, and there met a certain Lady Carsey.'

'But you did not tell her I was here!' cried Hannah.

'Thanks to Benjamin's well-talked-about exploits in the prize-ring, I am afraid she knows.'

Benjamin closed his eyes and prayed fervently to the God in whom he only half believed to spare him from that dreadful woman.

'We cannot go to Dover now,' said Hannah. 'She will hire thugs to stop the coach. She will do *something.*'

'You cannot be frightened of a mere *woman,*' said William.

'I am not suggesting Lady Carsey herself is the danger,' said the earl, 'but the villains she may hire.'

'Then instead of going to Dover, we had better go back to London,' said Hannah.

The earl frowned. 'You leave a further difficulty. If the coach is attacked, the coachman and guard will be left alone but not the passengers. Villains are notorious fools and may decide that the captain here is Benjamin in disguise and that Mrs Conningham is you, Miss Pym.' Mrs Conningham let out a faint shriek.

'So,' went on the earl, 'would there be any problem in you all residing with me for a few days until she loses the scent?'

Mrs Conningham forgot about her waiting brother-in-law, not to mention her daughter's suitor. To stay with an earl in his home!

'I could send an express to Uncle Henry,' she said eagerly, 'and tell him of our delay.'

'And what of you, Captain?' asked the earl.

'I was returning to my regiment before I was due,' said the captain. 'A few more days will not make any difference to me.'

Abigail was sitting with her hands clasped and her eyes shining, looking as if she had just been reprieved from the scaffold. Hannah was glad that Mrs Conningham was obviously too

76

excited and honoured by the earl's invitation to notice the happiness in her daughter's face.

'Well, William and I don't want to stay with you,' said Deborah.

The earl smiled at her sweetly. 'You were not even asked.'

William thought furiously. He felt he was being left out of an adventure. He was disappointed not to be going to Dover after all, for he had just remembered the name and address of an old friend who resided there. And then he had a marvellous idea and his eyes began to dance. While the earl was talking to the others and saying he would go home and send carriages for them, he whispered to his sister, 'Get Miss Pym's tickets for the coach before you leave.'

'Why?'

'I have a great plan,' muttered William. 'Do it and I promise you the adventure of a lifetime.'

Deborah grinned and the earl looked at the twins suspiciously.

The earl then left to make the arrangements. 'We had all best go to the booking-office and cancel our tickets,' said Hannah. William pressed Deborah's foot with his own under the table. 'My brother and I have a mind to go to Dover, Miss Pym,' said Deborah. 'I will be glad to pay you for your tickets.'

'My dear Lady Deborah,' said Hannah,

77

aghast, 'what if that monstrous woman has hired someone to hold up the coach?'

'They won't be looking for us,' said Deborah with a laugh. 'After all, does my brother look like a servant?'

'No. But nonetheless. . .'

'Oh, please do, Miss Pym,' said William, 'for we are determined to go.'

'Very well.' Hannah opened her reticule and took out two tickets. 'You will need to change Benjamin's,' she pointed out. 'It is an outside ticket. I meant to change it to an inside one, for the lad got a cruel soaking travelling on the roof.'

'We shall change it.' Deborah took the tickets and handed them to William.

'And none of you tell Ashton where we have gone,' warned Deborah. 'He is nothing to do with us.'

The captain shrugged in a way that indicated he did not care what they did and gave his promise, followed by Abigail and then her mother, who was only interested in getting to the earl's home. Hannah demurred for a bit but was overcome by the twins' protestations that they would be careful.

'Now what was that all about?' asked Deborah as she and her brother made their way home.

'Don't you see? It'll be a prime lark.' William's eyes glowed in the light from the carriage lamps. 'You dress in something plain and spinsterish and I will borrow a livery from one of our footmen. Lady Carsey'll think we're Miss Pym and Benjamin. We'll give her such a fright.'

'But the general opinion appears to be that Lady Carsey will not attack the coach in person,' said Deborah doubtfully.

'So?' demanded William. 'Two villains? Three? And with us both armed?'

For the first time in her life Deborah began to feel weak and womanly. She had followed William over hill and style and hedge since she could toddle. She had ridden with him on the hunting field, shot with him and shared his every exploit. And yet something in her quailed at the thought of confronting two, possibly three, armed men. But she could not bring herself to say so, for here was the ideal opportunity to help William forget that odious Clarissa. Clarissa would never dream of having adventures. Clarissa would scream and faint. So she fought down her misgivings and joined in the plans William was making.

* * *

The earl's guests had all retired for the night, but not one of them was asleep. Captain Beltravers stretched out in his comfortable bed and looked idly round at the rich if antique furnishings of the room. The bed in which he lay was a Jacobean one, ornately carved. The fireplace had a huge stone overmantel and pillars of knights in armour. The sheets were of the finest linen and scented with lavender. A brisk fire was setting shadows dancing around the room and sparking golden light from the brass-bound jugs of water which stood on a toilet-table, also laden with the finest pomades and soaps. The great house was hushed. Only the rich could afford that pleasant and tranquil quiet.

The captain reflected bitterly that he himself could have purchased a small but neat manor and could have lived in relative comfort if he had chosen to do so. His notoriously tight-fisted father had died shortly after the death of the captain's wife and child. The captain had promptly sold his childhood home, where he had never been happy, and the lands that went with it. He found himself possessed of a small fortune, but with no will to do anything with it. The death of his wife and beloved child had left him a shell of a man. But he had cried at last over their passing and with those tears had come calm relief. He was deeply grateful to Abigail Conningham.

He thought of her with affection. She should not be forced into a marriage with a man twice her age, a man she had never even met. She would make a good wife. He stared up at the embroidered canopy above his head, seeing not it, but a vision of a trim, shining house, and coming home in the evening and finding someone like Abigail waiting.

He was sure he could easily persuade that wretched uncle of hers to forget his plans for her. But he was rushing too far ahead. He would need to get to know her better. No one could replace his Mary in his heart, but Abigail had been right—he was sick to death of a military life and ready to begin a new one.

Abigail lay awake as well, wondering feverishly if Miss Pym had thought of anything. After all, it was so easy to say 'I will help,' and not *do* anything.

She thought of the captain rather dismally. He would never think of her other than as a friend. He was still wrapped up in the memory of his wife. But this stay at the earl's was a blessing. She would walk with him and talk with him and store up each precious memory to succour her in the bleak days and years that lay ahead. She shifted restlessly. The glory of Ashton Park could not make up for the prospect of Dover. She wondered whether Miss Pym was asleep or not. She got up and found a wrapper and crept out into the corridor. She would just scratch at Miss Pym's door and if there was no reply, she would return to bed.

Mrs Conningham was awake also, memorizing each rich item in the room to tell her friends when she returned to London. To the earl, his ancestral home might seem bleak and badly in need of modernizing, but to Mrs

Conningham it was all that a stately home should be: ancient retainers, great carved beds, suits of armour, and long dark twisting corridors hung with ancestral portraits. The maid who had prepared Mrs Conningham for bed had been so old, she had made Mrs Conningham feel quite youthful. Of course, it was a pity Abigail was taking things so badly, but she would soon settle down, as Mrs Conningham herself had had to learn to settle down after her parents had chosen a husband for her. There was too much sensibility and romanticism in this new century. Love and marriage should never be mixed up. A woman's duty in life was to bear as many children as possible and keep a comfortable home.

Mrs Conningham's fears that the captain might have any romantic interest in her daughter had been allayed. He had been polite, almost formal, towards Abigail at supper, nothing to fear there. Like most of the British public, Mrs Conningham despised the British army. Many inns carried signs saying, 'No redcoats.' She composed herself for sleep. The earl had promised to send her letter to Henry telling him of the delay. She hoped Jane was behaving herself and looking after the other children.

Hannah Pym tossed and turned. Her conscience was bothering her. She had not had an opportunity to tell Abigail of that letter to sister Jane. And now, if Jane left immediately as instructed, she would be in Dover before her mother and Abigail. And what of Lord William and Lady Deborah? She had allowed them to go off into possible danger without warning the earl. She should never have given that promise.

She rang the bell beside the bed and Benjamin, who was in a little bedchamber adjoining her own, came staggering in sleepily, dressed in his night-shirt.

'Benjamin!' said Hannah, sitting up. 'I cannot sleep. Jane Conningham will be in Dover before her mother and sister. I should never have interfered. And what of Lady Deborah and her brother, William? Why did I promise Lord William I would say nothing!'

Benjamin scratched himself lazily and then let out a cavernous yawn. 'I think,' he said blearily, 'that Miss Jane Conningham, if she be like other sisters, might have an interest in pinching her sister's beau. I would not trouble about it. And as for Lord William and Lady Deborah, why, I didn't promise to say nuffink, now did I?'

'Oh, Benjamin, how true. Write a note and put it under the earl's door. Who's there?'

There came a timid scratching on the bedroom door. Benjamin opened it. Abigail blushed scarlet at the sight of the footman in his night-wear and Benjamin darted behind a chair, using the back of it as a shield. 'You may

83

leave us, Benjamin,' said Hannah, 'and pray write that letter before you fall asleep.'

Benjamin grabbed Hannah's travelling writing-case and darted off to his own room.

'Now, Miss Abigail,' said Hannah, 'how may I be of service to you?'

Abigail sat down gingerly. 'I wondered whether you had time to hit on an idea.'

'Yes,' said Hannah, 'but I do not know whether it will do any good. I have sent money to your sister, Jane, with instructions she is to make her way to Dover at all speed.'

'But why?' wailed Abigail.

'The way I see it,' said Hannah, 'is that Miss Jane, having thought you a fool for not wanting to accept Mr Clegg, may try to get him for herself.'

Abigail sat frowning and then her face cleared. 'Oh, but of course she will. She is like that. And she is most monstrous jealous of me. I must tell Mama.'

'No, you must not,' said Hannah firmly. 'Only think. She might send another letter ahead to say that you are pining to see Mr Clegg or some such thing. People do not like to be crossed, particularly matchmaking mamas once their minds are made up.'

'You have given me hope,' said Abigail.

Hannah felt a stab of conscience. Abigail's eyes were full of admiration. But the idea had been Benjamin's. But were she to tell Abigail that, Abigail might decide it to be a disastrous plan. In straitened circumstances she might be, yet she still belonged to a class who considered servants had no brains to speak of.

'And now I think we should both get some sleep,' Hannah affected a yawn. She wanted to make sure Benjamin had written that note to the earl.

'You are so lucky to have a footman,' said Abigail wistfully. 'We had two, then one, then none. It does lower one's consequence so dreadfully not to have a footman. But I am surprised your maid does not travel with you.'

'Got the cold,' said Hannah.

Abigail rose and look her leave. Hannah went through to Benjamin's bedchamber. He said he was just finishing the note. Hannah retired satisfied. She had done all she could do. Benjamin was a good lad, and better than that, he was a footman.

People set more store by footmen than they did by *maîtres d'hôtel,* house stewards, masters of the horse, grooms of the chamber, valets, butlers, under-butlers, clerks of the kitchen, confectioners, cooks or any other of the miscellaneous assortment of servants that usually graces a large establishment. For footmen were definitely the lotus eaters of the servant class. Hannah's admonitions to Benjamin that a footman's duties included humble housewifery reflected on her own skills as a first-class housekeeper. Once the butler had gone, along with some other servants who were never replaced, Hannah had had the management of the footmen at Thornton Hall and had made sure they did their fair share of the work. But in grand households, footmen were there simply as a reflection of the wealth of the master. They were chosen as carefully as horses, for height, strength and appearance. The other servants on their time off dressed like ordinary civilians, but footmen hardly ever put off their grand livery, usually being as proud as peacocks and preferring to strut the streets in the glory of plush breeches, braided coat and powdered hair, rather than stoop to dressing like ordinary mortals. A lady with a footman in attendance, Hannah knew, made people think that she must come from a household full of servants, for in hard times, the gorgeous footmen were the first to go.

Before Hannah finally went to sleep, she wondered uneasily whether Lady Carsey planned any attack and hoped the Earl of Ashton could get the irrepressible twins off the stage-coach before they ran into danger.

*   *   *

Lady Carsey, lying in bed in one of the Langfords' guest bedchambers, was not asleep. She had felt fate was looking after her by sending that horrible Pym woman and Benjamin into her reach. As the earl had correctly guessed, she had no intention of mounting any attack herself. Men would have to be hired. But then, there was the question of money.

Like most landowners who managed their estates badly, Lady Carsey could not understand why she was suddenly short of money. She employed an agent, and when she needed money, it was the agent's duty to screw even more money out of the tenants. Not being in the slightest interested in the welfare of her tenants or in any agriculture whatsoever, it was enough for Lady Carsey when she rode out on her estates to think that all the land as far as she could see was hers. She did not care whether the land was growing gorse or grass, wheat or weeds. To a practised eye, the condition of her estates would spell ruin. There was the worn-out character of the soil, the poverty-stricken appearance of the tenants, and the dilapidated state of the farm buildings. The hedges were wild, the roads were dangerous in summer and impassable in winter. Knowing nothing of the land, Lady Carsey had long been convinced it would pay anything and it was her agent's duty to fill the voracious maw of her purse. But badly managed estates, like badly managed countries, have a way of suddenly collapsing all at once, or rather, that is how it looks to the one responsible for the neglect. So as the tenants left for other pastures, as the land yielded less and less, so Lady Carsey found that the well had dried up.

There was nothing else to be done, she thought, but to find herself a rich husband. To that end she had invited herself and her nephew, Mr Fotheringay, to the Langfords', having heard that the Langfords were friends of the unmarried Earl of Ashton. Although her nephew had stolen money from her before, she had managed to catch up with him before he had spent it, shaken it out of him, and become on friendly terms with him again. He was a weak, shiftless, dandified creature, and Lady Carsey needed someone to do her bidding. She accordingly rang for her maid and told the girl to fetch Mr Fotheringay.

The Exquisite presented himself half an hour later dressed in a huge quilted dressing-gown and wearing a turban on his head. The turban gave him a comical look, rather like one of the players in a pantomime who dress up in women's clothes and try to look as ungainly as possible.

'Yaas?' he demanded, sinking languidly into a chair.

'That Pym creature is here and her precious footman, Benjamin,' said Lady Carsey. 'Benjamin, would you believe it, won a purse at a prize-fight by flooring Randall.'

'I was there!' cried Mr Fotheringay. 'Capital sport. Didn't tell you 'cos I reckoned you'd had enough of him.'

'When you have ceased your enthusiastic burblings, you might recollect, my dear nephew, that I have a score to pay with that unlovely couple.'

'Oh, no,' said Mr Fotheringay with a delicate shudder. 'Remember what happened last time? That old witch, Pym, nearly burned your house down.'

'Exactly. And that is why I must get revenge but I must not be seen to be involved.'

Lady Carsey scowled horribly. Her standing in the town of Esher had diminished as rapidly as her money. It had got about quickly that her great wealth was nearly gone and no one fawned on her any more. She had not told her nephew of her financial troubles knowing that he hung around her in the hope of easy pickings. A rich woman could command great respect, could bribe officials, in those venal times, but a woman with the duns on her doorstep was another matter.

'I do not want to hire villains,' she said. 'That was disastrous last time. Pym and her creature are setting off at six in the morning on the stage-coach from the Crown. I want you to hold up that coach and rob them or shoot them. Whatever you will.'

'You're mad,' exclaimed Mr Fotheringay, startled out of his customary languor. 'I cannot hold up the stage-coach on the Dover road in broad daylight.'

'Then think of something,' said Lady Carsey angrily. 'I know. It is quite simple. There is no need for dramatics. They don't know what you look like. Get yourself a ticket on that coach. Do what you will. I'll give you poison. Put it in their grog at the first stop.'

'But the authorities will then question all on the coach.'

'And who is to know it's you? Disguise yourself and make yourself scarce once you have harmed them in some way.'

'Murder,' said Mr Fotheringay in a hollow voice. 'I can't do it.'

'I think you can. There is a slew of duns after you in London who would dearly like to know your whereabouts. And then you would have me to deal with.'

Mr Fotheringay bit his nails and looked at her out of the corner of his eyes. He was an evil creature but without the strength and boldness of his aunt. 'What's in it for me?' he asked.

'Ten thousand guineas.'

Mr Fotheringay stared at her in amazement, unaware that she could not hope to find such a sum and had no intention of paying him anyway.

'I like the poison idea,' he said. 'Do you have any?'

'Of course.'

'Silly of me to ask.'

'Besides,' said Lady Carsey, 'you have nothing to fear. People are dropping like flies all over England with one thing or the other. No local physician is going to trouble to open up their stomachs and try to diagnose whether they have been poisoned or not.'

'True, true,' agreed Mr Fotheringay, looking more cheerful, for he moved in a half-world where he knew well that relatives were conveniently poisoned for their money and often the perpetrators got away with it.

'And what will you be doing when I am off a-poisoning?' he asked acidly.

'Oh, I shall be planning how to seduce the Earl of Ashton.'

*   *   *

Deborah and William arose very early. Deborah put on a severe-looking grey gown and covered it with a blue wool cloak. On her head, she placed a sandy-coloured wig she had found in a hamper of props which had been used for amateur theatricals and, on top of that, a bonnet with a deep brim that concealed her face. William had borrowed a livery from one of the footmen. Over it he wore a greatcoat and one of the very latest in slouch hats, pulled down over his eyes. They both primed their pistols, William carrying his in one capacious pocket of his coat, and Deborah putting her smaller one in her reticule.

She had lost her fears of the night before. Now all it seemed like was a splendid adventure, and not for a moment would she admit to herself that that was because somewhere deep inside, she was sure Lady Carsey would not send anyone to attack the coach.

The mornings were light and the Dover road was busy. No highwayman had held up the Dover coach in broad daylight.

Her high spirits plunged when William said gaily, 'This will be an adventure to tell my Clarissa.'

'I would not do that,' said his sister acidly. 'She would scream and faint.'

'Right into my arms,' finished William, and began to whistle.

Deborah frowned, feeling uneasy. Her safe, carefree world was beginning to shake and tremble. Until the arrival of Clarissa, she had imagined she and William would always be together. She had not paid much serious attention to her father's threats to send her up to London for a Season. What was the good of having a splendid adventure if William was still going to think of Clarissa?

William called the coachman to bring the carriage round to take them to the inn. He told the butler that should the earl call, he was to say that Lady Deborah and Lord William were out fishing.

They arrived in the inn yard to find it full of bustle and noise. William changed his outside ticket for an inside one and then climbed into the repaired coach after his sister. The other passengers were a fussy old man who took snuff, a large lady of uncertain years wearing a bonnet with a huge pheasant's feather, a timid little girl who appeared to be the large lady's granddaughter, and a thin foppish man who scurried aboard the coach at the last minute with his head down and then sat darting curious glances this way and that. It was this last individual who made William cock a humorous eye at his sister and give her a nudge. 'What a guy,' he muttered.

Mr Fotheringay had chosen to attire himself as a huntsman, despite the fact that the season was over and he detested hunting. He was wearing a low narrow-collared coat which, although it was single-breasted, had a hole made on the button side to enable it to be kept together by means of a miniature snaffle. Under his coat was the broad ridge-and-furrow of a white cord waistcoat with a step collar, the vest reaching low down his figure, with large flap pockets and a nick out in front, like a coachman's. Instead of buttons, the waistcoat was secured with fox's tusks and catgut loops, with a heavy curb chain passing from one pocket to the other. His breeches came low down the leg and ended in a pair of what were called pork-butcher's boots—brown varnished things with thick soles. His spurs were bright and heavy, with formidable necks and rowels.

He was wearing a beaver hat with a curled brim and, belying the sportsmanlike appearance of his clothes, his face was painted.

His eyes fastened first on William's livery. 'Cold morning,' said Mr Fotheringay, rubbing his hands. 'But good hunting weather, for the scent will be high on such a morn.'

William raised his eyebrows superciliously.

'Got this one yesterday,' went on Mr Fotheringay, who, unlike most coach passengers, seemed eager to get into conversation. He brought a fox's brush out of his pocket and held it up. The large woman screamed and urged him to put it away.

'Yes, do,' agreed Deborah, 'for it does smell so dreadfully of moth-balls. You will be in bad odour with the farmers, sir, if you hunt out of season.'

Mr Fotheringay cursed under his breath. Never a huntsman and despising the breed, he had assumed they clattered across the fields all the year round.

He then affected surprise at the sight of William. 'Bless me!' he cried. 'Ain't you that fellow that trounced Randall?'

'The same,' said William and received a furious nudge from his sister, for his voice was cultured, well-modulated and hardly like Benjamin's tones, which swung between the coarse and the refined.

'By George, that was a fight,' cried Mr Fotheringay. 'Allow me to introduce meself. Name of Crank.'

Deborah stifled a giggle of laughter, but then the twins decided at the same time that the less they said, the better. 'Go to sleep, Benjamin,' said Deborah in what she hoped were the same rather authoritative bossy tones as Hannah Pym usually used.

'Yes, modom,' said William meekly and closed his eyes.

The coach, after rolling on for several miles with its now silent passengers, stopped briefly at Chatham. Mr Fotheringay fingered the bottle of poison in his pocket. A mixture of rum and milk was handed in to the passengers. No opportunity yet.

From Chatham the coach took that old Roman road, the old Watling Street, which ran as straight as an arrow. Both William and Deborah fell asleep, as did the other passengers, even Mr Fotheringay, who had become resigned to the idea of committing murder. Neither the Hannah Pym facing him nor her footman were as he remembered them was his last sleepy worry, and surely Benjamin, whom he had recently seen in the prize-ring, was older and taller? But he had checked at the booking-office to confirm they were on the coach. The Pym one had sandy hair poking out from below a hideous bonnet, just as he remembered, and Benjamin was in livery.

* * *

The Earl of Ashton awoke early, looked at the clock, yawned, turned over and went to sleep

95

again. He had not had a long lie in bed in ages.

He awoke properly at ten in the morning and looked at the clock in amazement before ringing the bell and summoning his valet.

'I hope my guests are not up and about,' he said.

'Only Miss Pym,' said the valet. 'The lady has gone for a walk about the grounds. I found this note on the floor earlier, my lord.'

The earl looked at it in surprise. It was in the shape of a cocked hat, the sort of note ladies usually send to gentlemen. He was used to being pursued and hoped Miss Conningham had not had the temerity to write to him.

'Get my shaving water ready,' he ordered. 'And put that down. I will read it later.'

At last shaved and washed and dressed, he picked up the note and opened it. He read what Benjamin had written and then cursed loudly.

He ran down the stairs and into the hall, shouting for his horse.

To make sure, he rode all the way to Downs Abbey, feeling considerably cooler by the time he arrived. Lady Carsey's thugs, if she had hired any, could not possibly mistake two golden-haired aristocrats, brother and sister, for Miss Pym and Benjamin. They would get a well-deserved fright, that was all. Nonetheless, he dismounted and walked into the hall and was soon questioning the old butler, Silvers.

Silvers inclined his head and said gravely

that my lord and my lady had gone out fishing. 'You have ridden hard, my lord,' said Silvers. 'Would you care to take some refreshment?'

The earl hesitated, but reminded himself that the coach was long gone and he had had no breakfast. 'I would like some coffee, Silvers, and something to eat.'

'Very good, my lord.' The butler led the way to a morning-room on the ground floor and threw open the door.

'We shall serve you breakfast directly, my lord.'

The earl sat down at the table. Then his eye fell on a large hamper standing against the wall. He got up and opened it. It was full of a mixture of clothes and wigs and grease-paint. He wondered whether the twins played charades of an evening. And what was such a thing doing in the breakfast-room?

The morning papers were brought in by a footman and handed to him. He opened one and then stared across it at the retreating footman, who was wearing a plain brown jacket and buff breeches.

'Where is your livery?' demanded the earl sharply, hoping that the servants were not taking their master's absence as an excuse to slack off.

The footman looked at the floor. To the suddenly suspicious earl he seemed to be thinking hard. Then the footman's eye fell on the hamper and his face cleared. 'My lord and my lady were set on putting up a little play,' he said. 'It has a footman in it, so Lord William asked if he could borrow my livery.'

'Oh, he did, did he?' The earl threw down his newspaper and made for the door. 'Tell Silvers I shall not be staying,' he said over his shoulder. He must try to catch that coach!

5

I wish, sir, you would practise this without me. I can't stay dying here all night.
Richard Brinsley Sheridan

The Dover coach rumbled on, passing through Rainham, Moor Street, Newington and finally rolled into Sittingbourne, where the travellers were to breakfast.

The sleepy twins awoke to the fact that they were both feeling jaded and gritty, that no one had held up the coach, and the dawning realization that no one was likely to.

Sittingbourne was a depressing town. It had started to rain, a thin, greasy drizzle. Deborah and William had only ever visited posting-houses, and the best ones at that. They had never, before their supper at the Crown in Rochester, patronized any hostelry which catered to stage-coach passengers. But the fare at the Crown had been very good. The food at the Bear at Sittingbourne proved to be quite another matter.

The insiders sat at a round table, except William, who suddenly remembered he was a footman, and stood behind his sister's chair.

'My footman is exhausted after his efforts at the prize-fight,' said Deborah. 'You may join us at table, Benjamin.'

Mr Fotheringay made space for William, so that he was sitting between the twins.

He fingered the bottle of poison in his pocket. What kind of poison was it? He felt squeamish. He hoped they would die quietly. But how to administer it?

Coffee was served along with the greasy breakfast. Deborah toyed with her food and studied a vast painting hung opposite the table. It depicted a rural scene, but it was so badly executed, it was hard to distinguish whether the figures in it were dancing or assaulting one another.

Mr Fotheringay gently eased the stopper from the bottle in his pocket. 'Look!' he cried suddenly. 'Is that not the Prince of Wales's coach arriving?'

People rushed to the door. Others, like William, stood up and craned their necks. Deborah, uninterested in the Prince of Wales and still staring moodily at the picture and wishing she had not come, saw the table reflected in the glass and saw the huntsman deftly pour the contents of a little bottle into her coffee-cup and then William's.

Her heart began to hammer. She did not believe this action had anything to do with Lady Carsey, but thought the huntsman, Mr Crank, was attempting to drug them. Of course. He thought William was Benjamin and was after the prize-money.

When the others returned, complaining there had been no coach of any kind arriving, Deborah suddenly cried out, 'But there are the Runners.'

Now it was Mr Fotheringay's turn to run to the door. Deborah quickly switched her coffee-cup for Mr Fotheringay's. For a moment, Mr Fotheringay thought he would die of fright, for there was a man in a red waistcoat strutting about the yard, but he finally realized that, despite the red waistcoat, the man was not one of the famous Bow Street Runners, come to take him to justice.

He returned to the table shaking his head. 'You are mistook, quite mistook,' he drawled. He turned to Deborah. 'But you do not drink your coffee?'

'It looks like sludge,' said William, who had been warned by Deborah. 'You drink yours first, sir, and tell us if it is palatable.'

'By all means.' Mr Fotheringay picked up his cup and drank the contents. 'Excellent,' he said, although he thought it had tasted decidedly nasty.

Deborah was feeling almost ill with nerves.

And then into the inn dining-room strode the Earl of Ashton.

'I want to speak to you two—*now,*' he commanded. He had expected an altercation, but to his surprise both rose meekly and followed him out. 'Have you gone mad?' demanded the earl. 'You could have been in danger.'

'We wanted an adventure,' said Deborah in a little voice. She had no intention of telling the earl about the huntsman and that mysterious bottle, but the reflection had been dim and now she was sure her strung-up nerves had been making her imagine things.

'I think the best thing both of you can do,' snapped the earl, 'is go and sit in the inn and I will cancel your tickets, hire a chaise, and take you both home.'

'Very good,' said William meekly.

The earl stared at them in surprise, not expecting acquiescence.

William and Deborah, with heads bowed, went back to the inn dining-room.

'Where is the huntsman?' asked Deborah.

'Gone out to the necessary house,' said the large woman. 'Feeling poorly.'

'Back in a minute,' muttered William. He ran out of the back of the inn and into the garden where the necessary house, or privy, stood at the end. From it came the terrible noise of retching.

He wrenched open the door. Mr

Fotheringay was kneeling in front of the wooden seat, making himself sick. William waited until the next spasm had passed and said coolly, 'That'll teach you to try to drug us, you villain.'

Mr Fotheringay turned a sweating, green face up to him. The poison had been an overdose of chloral, but he had managed to get rid of most of it. 'I knew what you'd done,' he whispered, 'when I began to get dizzy.' William was standing with his slouch hat in his hand, his guinea gold curls gleaming faintly in the gloom. 'You're not Benjamin,' cried Mr Fotheringay.

'No,' said William, 'and my sister ain't Miss Pym either.'

'Don't tell her I've failed,' begged Mr Fotheringay.

The light dawned. 'Lady Carsey?' asked William.

He nodded.

'I should turn you over to the nearest magistrate,' pointed out William.

Mr Fotheringay rallied slightly. 'What good would that do? I would swear you was fantasizing and I'd simply been taken ill. No proof.'

William stood for a long moment. Mr Fotheringay was desperately ill again.

'Who are you?' demanded William.

'Mind your own business.'

William seized him by his neckcloth

and jerked him upright, thrust a hand into his pocket and pulled out some letters, all addressed to Mr Fotheringay.

'So now I know who you are,' said William fiercely. 'I don't want any scandal.' He thought quickly. This Fotheringay must have got rid of the bottle of poison somewhere. There was, as he had said, no proof. It would come out in court that he, William, and his sister had been travelling on the stage because they thought Miss Pym and her footman were going to be attacked by Lady Carsey's henchmen. It would all sound mad. It would get in the newspapers and Clarissa would read about it.

He let go of Mr Fotheringay, who slumped to the earthen floor. William bent down and said fiercely, 'Do not come near Miss Pym again. If I see you anywhere in her vicinity, I will kill you. Understood?'

Mr Fotheringay nodded weakly.

William stalked off and Mr Fotheringay remained where he was on the floor of the privy and began to cry. After a while, he heard someone calling, 'Mr Crank. Coach leaving.' He remembered his pseudonym, struggled out and said to the landlord's wife, who was looking for him, 'I am feeling too poorly to continue my journey. I need a room and a bed.'

Soon he was safely tucked up in bed in an inn bedchamber with a hot brick at his feet. He was beginning to feel quite light-hearted. It was not the first time he had narrowly escaped death. The half-world of criminals and seedy young men he usually inhabited was full of violence.

And why should his aunt, Lady Carsey, know he had failed? If that horrible young man and his sister told her anything, then it was too bad, but he intended to keep away from her anyway. But if they did not, and she believed him to have committed the deed, then she might send him the money. He rang for pen, ink and paper and wrote her a letter saying he had successfully done what she had commanded and would she forward the money she had promised to the Bear Inn in Sittingbourne. He sealed it, handed it to a waiter and told him to put it on the next up mail coach.

Meanwhile, Deborah and William were being driven back toward Rochester by the Earl of Ashton in a comfortable post-chaise. Deborah was feeling very low. She wondered what had happened to the mysterious Mr Crank, but could not say anything in front of the earl.

The earl, for his part, had received such a humble apology from William that he was feeling indulgent towards the pair of them. They were little more than children, he reflected. He thought uneasily of the violent feelings he had experienced when he had kissed Lady Deborah, but then gave a mental shrug and decided he had been celibate too long. He talked to them lightly, but rather like an uncle. Deborah felt very depressed and removed her ugly bonnet and took off her wig and ran her fingers through her thick blonde curls, one of the first feminine gestures William had ever seen her make.

At Downs Abbey, the earl refused to enter the house, saying he must return home and see how his guests were faring. 'And I had better go and see Langford,' he added, 'and warn him about Lady Carsey. She should not be allowed to remain under his roof.'

He ruffled Deborah's curls just as if she were a child and smiled in a kindly way. 'You are a dreadful scamp,' he said with a grin, 'and the sooner your father is home to take care of you, the easier I shall feel.'

The twins waited until he had left and went indoors. William seized Deborah's arm and dragged her into the morning-room. 'What happened?' demanded Deborah.

William told her while Deborah's eyes widened in alarm. 'I could have killed him, William, and how could I ever have lived with that?'

'Well, you didn't,' said William crossly. 'But you see, Deb, I couldn't make a scandal and what proof do we have?' He did not know Mr Fotheringay was Lady Carsey's nephew, assuming from Mr Fotheringay's dreadful dress that he was some thug she had hired. 'He seemed more frightened of Lady Carsey than the law and swore he would simply say he had been taken unwell. And what guys we would look! And what would Clarissa think if she saw it in the newspapers?'

'A pox on Clarissa!' shouted the overwrought Deborah.

'Watch your trap,' snapped William. Deborah turned her face away to hide the sudden rush of tears.

When had she and William ever quarrelled before?

'Hey, Deb!' cried William suddenly. 'I have a plan.'

She turned to face him, glad the brief row was over.

'What plan?'

'This Lady Carsey is at Langford's. He'll send her packing, but she'll probably be there tonight. You remember Langford's place and how the cook used to spoil us, you know, that door at the side where we'd creep in and find our way down to the kitchens?'

'Yes, what of it?'

'We'll go over tonight and *haunt* her, you as Miss Pym and me as Benjamin. Woo! Hoooo! Wooo!' cried William, waving his arms and jumping up and down.

But somewhere on the road back from Sittingbourne, under the earl's tolerant, avuncular eye, Lady Deborah had left the last remnant of her childhood behind.

She sat down wearily. 'Don't be tiresome, William. It's a stupid idea.'

'It's a first-rate idea,' raged William. 'I'll go myself, if you've turned coward.'

'I have not turned coward,' said Deborah hotly. 'But what if it goes wrong and Ashton learns of it? He'll write to the embassy in Turkey and tell Papa to come home.'

'How would he find out about it? What has happened to you, Deb? You used to be *fun.*'

'Oh, I'll go, I'll go,' said Deborah, terrified of losing her beloved brother's affection.

'Good, that's more like you,' said William with satisfaction. 'Why should that horrible, horrible woman come out of this without even a fright?'

* * *

The Earl of Ashton was aware of a difference in his home as soon as he walked into the hall. A fire was burning brightly in the huge hall fireplace, for the day had turned chilly, although he could not, now he came to think of it, remember having seen a welcoming fire in the hall before. Then, on a side-table, was an exquisite arrangement of flowers.

Hannah Pym had taken over. He did not yet know that, only that the great mansion seemed less drab and dingy than usual.

He changed out of his riding-clothes and went down to the drawing-room. Again, there were flowers everywhere and the pleasant scent of wax candles. Hannah was reading, Mrs Conningham was sewing, Abigail was playing the piano, and the captain was standing beside her, turning the pages.

'I am sorry I had to leave you,' said the earl, sitting down on a chair next to Hannah. 'That wretched pair, Lord William and Lady Deborah, went off in the coach, masquerading as you and your footman. It was Sittingbourne before I caught up with them and brought them back.'

'How could they do such a thing?' demanded Hannah, very cross that Lady Deborah should continue to behave like a tomboy. For a short while it had looked to Hannah's matchmaking eye as if there might be a chance that the earl would become romantically interested in Lady Deborah.

'They are little more than children,' said the earl with an indulgent laugh. 'Now I must leave you again, Miss Pym, for I feel it my duty to ride over and tell Langford about Lady Carsey. He should not have such a creature under his roof.'

His journey, had he but known it, was not really necessary. Lady Carsey had already been told to leave, Sir Paul Langford and his lady giving the usual excuse to speed the unwanted guest by saying that they were leaving on a visit elsewhere. Lady Carsey had fallen victim to the lady's-maid grapevine.

When it came to relating gossip abovestairs, the lady's-maids were quite a power. Lady Carsey had a new lady's maid, Francine, a flighty creature who had taken a dislike to her mistress shortly after she was engaged. But she was clever and sly and pretended to dote on her. From Lady Carsey's other servants, particularly the ones she had dismissed, she had quickly learned all the scandals connected with her mistress and, by flirting with the estate agent, had found out about Lady Carsey's ruin.

But an impoverished mistress was something to be kept quiet about, as any of Lady Carsey's servants would lose consequence as a result of it, and so Francine had kept all she knew to herself. But that morning, Lady Carsey had been in a foul temper. She had taken to drinking heavily but concealed it well. She vaguely remembered sending John Fotheringay off to murder Miss Pym and Benjamin, and, in the cold light of day and with a pounding headache, she wondered if she had run mad. Great wealth was a good protection against the law of the land. England, unlike France, refused to countenance a police force, and so the law was carried out by Bow Street Runners, who were more like thieves themselves, and parish constables who did their duty for only a month before handing over to someone else who equally resented the duty, and the elderly men of the watch, who were often too old and infirm to be interested in anything other than staying alive.

So when Francine clumsily dropped a scent bottle and the smell of the spilt contents crept around the room, making Lady Carsey feel even more ill, she unleashed the worst of her temper on the lady's-maid for the first time.

Francine sponged up the mess, opened the windows, and then went down to the servants' hall and proceeded to murder her mistress's reputation. She told of the attempt to have Benjamin tried and hanged for a theft he did not commit, of his subsequent abduction, and ended with saying that Lady Carsey had left to visit the Langfords to get away from the duns on her doorstep.

Lady Langford's lady's-maid, Betty, told her mistress the whole while dressing her head with flowers and feathers. Appalled, Lady Langford sent for her husband, who gave her the usual lecture about listening to servants' gossip, and then proceeded to discuss with his wife the best way of speeding the parting guest.

'Tell her we're off to stay with the Chawleys tomorrow,' said Lady Langford, 'and she'll need to leave first thing in the morning.'

Lady Carsey was feeling much restored by the time she descended to the drawing-room to pass that tedious country-house time before dinner. One of the other guests, a Mr

Frederick Jolly, was sitting on a sofa staring into space.

Lady Carsey sat down next to him. He was a fish-faced young dandy who looked as if he had been blown into his clothes, they were so very tight and so very shiny. He was corseted and padded and nip-waisted and painted, and so dead-faced, he looked like a dummy.

'The weather has been unseasonably cold,' essayed Lady Carsey.

'Yaas,' he said, staring straight ahead. 'The weather has been unseasonably cold.'

'Do you live in this county?' pursued Lady Carsey.

'No, I do not live in this county,' replied Mr Jolly.

Lady Carsey gave a sigh and rose and went to join old Lord Rothers, who was stooped over the fire. He was a short, square, ugly man like John Bull. 'How have you passed your day?' asked Lady Carsey gaily.

He gave her a terrified look, straightened up and bundled his great red hands into fists.

'Well. . . ahem . . . rumph! . . . don't you know. . . ahem. . . garrumph!'

'Quite,' said Lady Carsey faintly.

The door opened and Sir Paul and Lady Langford walked in. They stood on the threshold, very close together. 'Lady Carsey,' yelled Sir Paul, and then flushed and lowered his voice. 'Lady Carsey, we are going on a visit to the Chawleys in the morning. I am afraid you will have to leave first thing.'

'What a pity,' said Lady Carsey lightly.

Mr Jolly and Lord Rothers looked startled, recognizing the time-honoured way of getting rid of the unwanted and each wondering feverishly what they had done to offend. The Langfords had decided to sacrifice both of them in the good cause of getting shot of Lady Carsey.

The footmen came in with the before-dinner drinks. Now Lady Carsey was aware of an atmosphere of contempt, of unease. The footmen looked at her with bold curiosity instead of lowering their eyes as they were supposed to do before their betters, and Sir Paul and his lady were sitting as far away from Lady Carsey as they could get. There is nothing more abhorrent to the British aristocracy than the sight of someone in financial difficulties. Lady Carsey could have been rumoured to have been guilty of all sorts of skulduggery without raising the same disgust in the Langford soul.

Dinner was a poor affair, the Langfords having told their cook not to go to any special effort. Lady Carsey proceeded to drink too much. The two other guests were incapable of conversation and the Langfords seemed determined not to offer any. The butler came in with the bleached old mail-bag and began to hand out letters, saying the mail had just come up from Rochester.

Lady Carsey murmured an excuse and broke open the seal containing her nephew's letter. She could feel a clammy sweat breaking out on her brow. Miss Pym, she remembered, had powerful friends. Now she wanted the evening to end. But the butler reappeared to announce the arrival of the Earl of Ashton. Lady Carsey brightened, but her face fell when the butler added that Lord Ashton wished to see the master privately.

Sir Paul departed and returned half an hour later, looking grim. He told the gentlemen that they were welcome to sit up over their port but he himself had the headache and meant to lie down.

Soon Lady Carsey, fortified with a bottle of brandy, was back in her room again. She told Francine that they would leave in the morning and told that young lady to report for duty at six o'clock and begin to pack. Francine sulkily prepared her for bed and then flounced out, leaving her mistress to her thoughts and her brandy.

The more brandy Lady Carsey drank, the more she became convinced she could trap the Earl of Ashton. Instead of returning to Esher direct, she would call at his home on some pretext.

She had almost forgotten about Miss Pym and that footman. With a smile on her lips, she drifted off to sleep.

William and Deborah were down below in the Langfords' kitchens, sitting at the scrubbed deal table eating hot biscuits, baked for them by the old cook, who treated both the twins as if they were still the tousle-headed scamps who used to ride over to see her.

They were regaled with all the gossip about Lady Carsey and how she had been sent packing, and so William was able to find out that she was in the Blue Room, which was just off the back stairs.

Deborah, looking at her brother's flushed and happy face as he munched biscuits and teased the cook, thought that he appeared now like her younger brother. She did not want to go ahead with the masquerade, which stuck her now as horrible, while William appeared to think it was ajape. What would Ashton think if he found out? She had an impatient longing to see the earl treat her like an adult, a woman. She remembered the careless way he had ruffled her curls. That sweet and passionate kiss must have been sweet and passionate only on her side. He has probably kissed scores of women, thought Deborah, miserably crumbling a biscuit and wishing the night's escapade were over.

At last William rose to leave, with many promises to come again. They went quietly out into the grounds, but only as far as a gazebo a little way away from the house, where they had hidden their disguises.

Normally they would have talked and joked to pass the time, but Deborah kept falling silent. Perhaps, she thought guiltily, someone like Clarissa was just what her brother needed to make him grow up.

One by one, the candles and oil-lamps in the mansion were put out. The twins waited an hour longer, beginning to shiver with nerves and cold.

'Now,' said William, lighting a dark lantern, 'on with our disguises.'

Soon he was dressed in livery and with the slouched hat pulled down to hide his face. Deborah put on the sandy wig and a plain grey gown. 'We'll put the grease-paint on in the servants' hall. There's a mirror there,' said William.

They crept towards the house and in by the little-used door at the side which the butler always forgot to lock and made their way to the servants' hall. Fortunately for William and Deborah, the Langfords treated their servants well and there was no one sleeping on the floor.

They painted their faces with white grease-paint
and dusted their clothes down with flour. 'It's a pity there aren't any chains,' said William.

'It's just as well there aren't,' pointed out

Deborah. 'We have to get up the back stairs to her room *quietly.* Leave your shoes. We're not supposed to make a noise. What are you doing with that omelette pan?'

'Magnesium powder,' said William with a grin. 'We light this just when we finish our haunting. There'll be a tremendous flash. Got to light it in the pan and take the pan away with us so as to leave no clues that we are human.'

Lady Carsey had fallen into a heavy drunken sleep, which, like most heavy drunken sleeps, only lasted an hour. She began to twist and turn, beset with worries. Why had she sent John Fotheringay off to kill that pair? It had been different at Portsmouth, when he had hired smugglers to try to do the dirty work. Her own nephew! She sat up. If John were caught, then he would talk and talk.

Francine had made up the fire before she went to bed, and red flickering flames set the shadows dancing.

And then she distinctly heard a low moan. She put one white hand up to her throat and stared wildly around and then reached for the bell-pull beside the bed. But before she could even touch it, they were there in the shadowy corner of her room, two terrible figures, their faces blanched and white, their dark clothes outlined in white.

'Woooo!' said a sepulchral voice. 'I am Benjamin Stubbs, most foully murdered.'

116

'And I too. I am Hannah Pym,' wailed the female figure.

Lady Carsey opened her mouth to scream but no sound came out.

'We will haunt you until the day you die,' moaned the Benjamin ghost.

'Till you die,' echoed the Miss Pym ghost.

Like nearly everyone in this modern age of 1800, Lady Carsey still believed in ghosts. 'Go,' she whispered. 'It was a joke. A little chloral.'

'We will drag you down to hell,' said William. He was beginning to enjoy himself immensely. Then he thought he heard a footfall somewhere in the house. He motioned Deborah to stand in front of him and bent down and lit a taper at the fire.

'We will return,' he moaned and lit the magnesium powder. There was a hellish flash, William having been over-generous with the powder. Lady Carsey screamed and screamed as the twins made their escape.

Francine came running in, her lace nightcap askew. 'Ghosts,' whispered Lady Carsey. 'There. By the fire.'

'You've had a bad dream, my lady.'

'But the smoke. The foul smell of the pit.'

Francine wrinkled her small nose. A coal from the fire was lying smoking on the hearth. She picked it up with the tongs and put it back on the fire. 'Nothing but a burning coal, mem,' she said scornfully, and flapped at the smoke from the magnesium powder, which was still drifting about the room. 'I saw them, I tell you,' muttered Lady Carsey, her teeth chattering.

'Nobody there, mem,' said Francine. 'I tell you, you've had a bad dream.' She cast a speaking look at the nearly empty brandy bottle beside the bed.

'I *didn't*. They were there,' muttered Lady Carsey. 'I cannot be left alone this night. Get into bed with me.'

Francine backed away. She had heard all about Lady Carsey's odd tastes and, like most servants, learned more about sexual vagaries in her youth than most ladies would learn in a lifetime. 'Oh, no,' said Francine. 'You'll feel better in the morning,' and fled from the room.

Lady Carsey lay back against the pillows, trembling. She forced herself to rise and to light every candle in the room. Then she dressed and sat shivering, waiting desperately for daylight, when ghosts returned to their dark world.

*   *   *

'So,' said the Earl of Ashton the next morning at breakfast, 'I shall ride over to Rochester today and arrange seats for you all on the Dover coach which leaves the day after tomorrow. I do not think you are in any danger. The fact is, or so Langford tells me, that Lady Carsey has fallen on hard times and

118

will find it difficult to evade justice in future.'

'Another day,' said Abigail softly.

'Yes,' said her mother and then, deliberately misunderstanding her daughter, she added, 'My pet is anxious to meet her beau.'

Hannah noticed that the captain looked gloomy and Abigail miserable and hoped that sister Jane was the competitive minx that Abigail had led her to believe she was.

'Have you any objection to lending me one of your hunters?' asked the captain abruptly. 'I would like to take a ride about the estate. I have a mind to end my military days and purchase a little property of my own.'

Mrs Conningham put down the piece of toast she had been about to munch and stared at him. 'A ride around this magnificent estate will not give you any idea of how to run a cottage and garden,' she said.

The captain ignored her. 'I had in mind a tidy little estate, nothing like this, but with some good fishing and rough shooting.'

'Indeed!' The earl looked at him in surprise. 'Travers's place over at Spurry Ridge is due to go under the hammer. He's in sore need of funds and you could probably have it lock, stock and barrel for a bargain. Let me see, there's one hundred and fifty acres of quite good land, three farms in need of some cash being pumped into them, good stables and outbuildings. All Travers's money went on the hunt. Three thousand a year he spent on his hounds. Take my advice, Captain, and avoid hunting if you want to stay solvent.'

'And the house?' asked Captain Beltravers eagerly.

'Quite modern. Built around 1750. Good brick and no dry rot as I recall. Six bedchambers and, let me see, the usual —dining-room, drawing-room, saloon, muniments room, gun-room, library, and then all the usual servants' quarters, pantry and still-room, kitchens and so on. I'll take you over this afternoon, if you like. Beltravers! There was a Mr John Beltravers who had a tidy property at Deal.'

'My father,' said the captain curtly. 'I inherited the lot and sold it. My wife was dead, you see, and . . . well. . .'

'I understand,' said the earl sympathetically. 'In any case, it would pass the afternoon.'

'Would you care to come?' the captain asked Mrs Conningham.

'We should be delighted,' said Mrs Conningham, eyeing the captain with a look half-calculating, half-surprised.

'I am not a very good rider,' said Abigail timidly.

'We'll all go in my carriage,' said the earl. 'Miss Pym?'

Hannah smiled. 'I shall be quite happy having a quiet afternoon here in your beautiful home.' Hannah felt sure her presence would not be needed. Mrs Conningham had found out the captain had money. Let her see the house and let her begin to imagine the possibility of her daughter living there. Then she, Hannah Pym, would get to work on her when the party returned.

*   *   *

The earl returned at midday with the coach tickets he had insisted on paying for, and then set off in his carriage with the captain, Mrs Conningham and her daughter. Hannah watched them go. Abigail's pelisse and gown were sadly dashed and no man liked a girl in a dashed gown, thought Hannah. They expected everything to be bandbox fresh. Nothing she had herself would fit Abigail.

She was just about to send for Benjamin and take a walk when Lady Deborah and Lord William were announced. Hannah rose to greet them, noticing with quick eyes that William appeared to take the news that Lord Ashton was absent with equanimity, but his sister looked a trifle put out. Also, Deborah was wearing a handsome carriage dress of blue velvet, the colour of her eyes, and a very modish bonnet.

'Lord Ashton was most upset when he learned you had gone off on the coach,' said Hannah. 'You are lucky you did not come to any harm.'

'Pooh. It was all so tedious,' said Deborah,

flashing her brother a warning look. 'Perhaps Lady Carsey found her long-lost conscience.'

'Such as she was born without one,' remarked Hannah tartly. She studied Deborah's handsome dress again and then her eyes glowed green. It was time in any case that Lady Deborah forgot her hoydenish ways and settled down to becoming a lady. 'What a splendid gown, Lady Deborah,' said Hannah. 'I was led to believe that you did not care for frills and furbelows.'

'She wouldn't if left to herself,' laughed William. 'Papa gets a London dressmaker to make up the latest.'

'It is just that I cannot help hoping you might assist me in a plot to further a romance,' ventured Hannah. Deborah looked amused while William snorted in disgust, his feelings for Clarissa not having made him view the idea of anyone else's romance with a kinder eye.

'If I can,' said Deborah cautiously.

'I wish to help Miss Conningham, Miss Abigail Conningham. You met at the Crown?'

Both nodded.

'She is in sore distress because her uncle in Dover has picked out a husband for her. The future husband is in his forties. She does not wish to marry this Mr Clegg. She does, however, favour Captain Beltravers, who is part of our coach party. The captain, thanks to Miss Conningham, has decided to leave the army, buy a tidy property and settle down. To that end, Lord Ashton has taken him to look at a place for sale, I believe, by a Mr Travers.'

'The captain must have a tidy bit put by,' exclaimed William.

'Exactly. But the problem is this. The captain still mourns his late wife. Mrs Cunningham has learned that the captain has money and will look on him with a favourable eye. Oh, I should have gone with them!'

'Why?' asked Deborah.

'For I now realize that Mrs Conningham will look on our captain with *too* favourable an eye. The daughter will no longer be forbidden fruit. She is plain and could look considerably better with a little help. She went off wearing a gown and pelisse that had seen better days.'

'Dashed?' asked Deborah sympathetically.

'Very dashed. Also, she has a muddy brown-coloured silk with the waist at the waistline instead of up under the arms where it should be. She will no doubt wear it at dinner. Mrs Conningham will gush over the captain. Abigail will be crushed.'

'And where do I feature in your matchmaking?' asked Deborah.

'Perhaps you could lend Miss Abigail a pretty gown.'

'Miss Pym! She would be most humiliated.'

'Not if you put it the right way. You could say, for instance, that her grand gowns are no doubt being sent on to Dover from London and you thought she might like to borrow something of yours, particularly as the earl is going to invite you for dinner.'

'He is?' asked the twins in unison.

'Oh, I'm sure he is,' said Hannah earnestly. 'I mean, if you were to pay a call about one hour before the dressing gong with the gown for Miss Conningham, he is bound to ask you to stay.'

'Won't he think it deuced odd if Debs and I call in all our evening finery?' asked William.

'Not at all,' said Hannah primly. 'You tell him you dine at home like that every evening.'

William roared with laughter. 'Famous! But I am afraid we can't be doing with such flummery, and the less I see of Ashton the better.'

'Miss Pym asked *me*,' said Deborah quietly, 'and yes, Miss Pym, I do have the very gown and I will bring it over along with some bits and pieces to embellish it.'

'I say,' said William crossly as they rode home, 'whatever are you about to promise that crooked-nosed Pym female to help in her meddling matchmaking? Now we'll have to get all titivated up and Ashton will no doubt bore us with a sermon over dinner.'

'Do as you like,' replied his sister indifferently. 'I shall most certainly go.' They rode on in silence, each with their own thoughts, the old closeness between them gone.

Hannah summoned Benjamin and said she would like to take a walk in the grounds and wished him to accompany her—'for you are becoming like all footmen, Benjamin, too fond of the butler's port and pantry and not enough of the fresh air.'

'Hardly a day for a walk, modom,' complained Benjamin when they were outside. Mist was rising from the ground and crawling snakelike around the bowls of the trees.

Hannah strode on, ignoring his remarks. 'Take deep breaths, Benjamin, and throw out your chest.'

'I 'ates the bleedin' country,' mumbled her footman from somewhere in the mist behind her. 'Fog an' bleedin' damp and poxy hanimals slaughterin' each uvver.'

Hannah thought it politic to ignore him. Despite the mist, the air was quite warm and pleasant, and somewhere above, the sun was trying to struggle through.

*   *   *

Lady Carsey had tumbled back into bed exhausted at dawn and did not wake until nearly noon. She recollected the events of the night before with a shudder and assumed she had had the Horrors, which was how the polite described delirium tremens, the curse of a hard-drinking society.

She was not surprised to find that her hosts had not left. Her bags were packed and her coach brought around. She did not tip any of the Langford servants and made Lady Langford a curt goodbye.

As she climbed into the coach, she ordered the coachman to drive her to Ashton Park. Her visit must not be wasted. She would think of some way in which to persuade the earl to let her stay the night.

Soon the coach was bowling up the long drive to Ashton Park. She peered out into the thickening mist, wishing she could see more of the property her optimistic mind was already beginning to regard as her own.

The butler told her solemnly that the earl and his guests had ridden out to the Travers's place.

'I am an old friend of his lordship. I shall wait,' said Lady Carsey grandly.

She was shown into the drawing-room and, after being served with tea and cakes, left to her own devices. She looked about her with a critical eye. The furniture was sadly old-fashioned, and moth had got into the curtains, but the carpet was good and an effort had been made to cheer the room with several excellent flower arrangements. There was a piece of discarded embroidery lying on the sofa. Lady Carsey frowned. That butler had said the earl had guests and obviously at least one of the

126

guests was female. A faint glow at the windows showed that the sun was beginning to shine through the mist. Hopeful of seeing something now of the park, she rose to her feet and walked to the windows and looked down.

The mist was still coiling around the trees, blown by a fitful breeze.

And then suddenly she saw them.

The ghosts of Hannah Pym and Benjamin Stubbs. Benjamin was in black velvet livery and Hannah had put on one of her old black housekeeper's gowns.

They were walking slowly, *gliding* across the grass. And then they disappeared.

Down below on the lawn, Hannah heard a plaintive miaow. She peered up into the branches of a tall oak tree. 'Benjamin,' she said, 'there is a kitty up there.'

'It'll come down if you leave it alone. Moggies allus do,' grumbled Benjamin.

'But it sounded such a *small* cat,' said Hannah, betraying once more how far she had moved from the servant class, for servants did not have the luxury of having tender thoughts about animals.

'Enjoying itself,' commented Benjamin repressively.

'Benjamin! I thought I had made myself clear. Go up that tree this minute and rescue that animal.'

Benjamin sighed but nipped up the broad branches of the tree like lightning.

The upper branches of the tree were on a level with the drawing-room windows, but over to the left, where the branches had been trimmed back so that they did not obscure the view of the park, Lady Carsey was still staring out, chalk-white and shaking.

She caught a little sign of movement to her left and looked straight into the face of Benjamin. Benjamin's face contorted with fear at the sight of her and he let out a wail.

Lady Carsey screamed and screamed. She blundered from the drawing-room, shouting desperately for her coach. She crouched in a corner of the hall while it was being brought round, babbling incoherently and making the sign of the cross. Francine tried to burn feathers under her nose, but Lady Carsey only screamed the harder and pushed her away.

When her coach arrived, she scrambled in and crouched on the floor and stayed there muttering and shaking until the coach was several miles away from Ashton Park.

Benjamin scrambled down the tree and handed Hannah a small fluffy kitten. 'You'll never guess, modom,' he panted. 'I looked in the drawing-room window and I saw 'er, Lady Carsey. She was as white as a sheet, like she'd seen a ghost.'

'Fustian!' said Hannah roundly. The sound of a hastily departing carriage reached their ears. Hannah quickened her step and entered the hall. All the old and creaking servants were gathered there, talking excitedly.

Hannah was soon told about the strange visit of Lady Carsey and how she had suddenly gone mad and run off. 'How very odd,' said Hannah Pym. 'The woman must have a conscience after all, Benjamin, and when she saw you, she must have remembered how you were nearly hanged because of her spite and lost her wits!'

6

Anything awful makes me laugh.
I misbehaved once at a funeral.

Charles Lamb

Hannah knew that things had gone very badly for Abigail as soon as she saw the girl's sad face and her mother's excited one.

The captain looked withdrawn. Mrs Conningham was hanging on to his arm as they entered the hall of Ashton Park, chattering nineteen to the dozen. Was not that property sublime? Everything in perfect order and as neat as a pin. Of course—slyly—it lacked a woman's touch.

Right behind them came Deborah and William. The earl, startled, invited both for dinner, and all dispersed and went upstairs to the rooms allotted to them instead of gathering in the drawing-room to chat and await the ringing of the dressing-bell: Mrs Conningham because she was tired, and the captain because he was tired of Mrs Conningham; William and Deborah in case the earl might change his mind; and Hannah because she wanted to get to work on Abigail.

Deborah found Abigail lying face down on the bed, weeping.

'Now, now, Miss Conningham,' said Deborah, ringing the bell and telling the servant who answered it that Miss Pym must present herself as soon as possible. While she waited for Hannah, Deborah sat down on the edge of the bed and patted Abigail helplessly on the shoulder and wished she could find something to say other than, 'Now, now.'

Hannah Pym swept in and took in the situation at a glance.

'Dear me,' she cried, 'this will never do. Miss Conningham, you will ruin your looks with weeping. Come, sit up and let me bathe your face.' Her crisp voice had the effect of calming Abigail. She got up shakily and stood like an obedient child while Hannah sponged and dried her face.

'Now, let me guess,' said Hannah briskly. 'Your mama has found out the captain is in funds and has chosen to forget the existence of Mr Clegg. She gushed all over the captain and the more she gushed, the more silent and

130

withdrawn he became.'

'It. . . it. . . was *awful*,' gulped Abigail. 'He hardly spoke to me. At last, just before we were to leave, he looked around and said it would have been a wonderful place to bring up his boy.'

'Well, you will not repair the damage by looking like a wreck.' Hannah turned to Deborah. 'Did you bring the dress?'

'Yes, one of my prettiest.'

'Fetch it here,' commanded Hannah.

She took Abigail's hand and led her to a chair. 'I am going to talk to you very severely, my child. If something is worth fighting for, then you need to fight very hard, and you need a suit of armour. We were going to put this to you more delicately, but we do not have time. Lady Deborah has brought you a fine gown and you must look your best for the captain. We need not tell your mama of this. She will notice, of course, but you can say afterwards that Lady Deborah assumed all your grand gowns were being sent down to Dover from London and chose to lend you something. Goodness, look at the time!'

'But there are two whole hours to go before dinner!' exclaimed Abigail.

'And it will take all of that to get you in shape.' Hannah rolled up her sleeves. 'I will be your lady's-maid. Undress down to your shift and sit at the toilet-table.'

Deborah, returning with a small trunk

containing the gown, was pressed into service. Hannah was stirring up a wash for Abigail's face which she said was guaranteed to whiten the skin. 'I made this myself,' said Hannah. 'It consists of fifty parts milk of almonds mixed with rose-water and four parts aluminium sulphate. See that Miss Abigail bathes her face well, Lady Deborah, while I get the beauty cream.' Hannah bent over and began to rummage in a capacious bag of cosmetics she had brought with her.

'Do you make all your own cosmetics?' asked Deborah, amused that such a spinsterish and upright lady as Hannah Pym should be so conversant with beauty aids.

'Yes, Mrs Clarence taught me.'

'A friend of yours?'

'A good friend,' said Hannah, who had no intention of telling Lady Deborah that Mrs Clarence had been her employer. Yes, she had told previous aristocratic ladies she had met on her travels the truth, but she still did not know Lady Deborah very well.

'And how did you make this cream?' asked Deborah, peering into a large jar.

'It is made from,' said Hannah, 'ten grams of powdered alum, two whites of egg, three grams of boric acid, forty drops of tincture of benzoin, forty drops of olive oil, five drops of mucilage of acacia and a sufficient quantity of rice flour and perfume.

'You mix the alum with the white of egg,

132

without any addition of water whatsoever, in an earthen vessel and dissolve the alum with the aid of gentle heat from a small lamp, and with constant, even stirring. This must continue until the water content of the albumen is driven off. Care must be taken to avoid curdling of the albumen—which occurs very easily, as we all know. Let the mass obtained in this manner get completely cold, then throw it into a Wedgwood mortar, add the boric acid, tincture of benzoin, oil, mucilage et cetera, and rub up together, thickening it with the addition of rice flour to give the desired consistency, and perfuming as you go along.'

'Goodness!' exclaimed Deborah. 'It sounds like skin *remover!*'

'Nonsense,' snapped Hannah. 'She will look very beautiful.'

Deborah worked patiently under Hannah's instructions, laying the gown out on the bed, heating the little spirit stove and putting the curling tongs on it to heat, and passing Hannah jars and bottles out of her bag.

Deborah found it strangely soothing, the murmur of Hannah's voice as she worked away, the smell of the salves and creams and washes and pomatums, the closeness of three women working hard to trap a man.

She finally helped Hannah to slip the gown over Abigail's head and tie the tapes. The gown was of gossamer blue chiffon over a silk underdress of paler blue. It had little frills on the puffed sleeves, a deep neckline revealing that Abigail boasted an excellent bosom, and three deep, frilly flounces at the hem.

'And I brought you these things to set it off,' said Deborah, and Abigail cried in amazement as she produced a thin, delicate sapphire-and-gold necklace with two thin gold-and-sapphire bracelets, a headdress of blue silk cornflowers, and a pair of long white kid gloves.

Abigail was made to sit down in front of the mirror again while the headdress was tenderly placed on her freshly curled and pomaded hair. Hannah studied her critically and then brought some lampblack and proceeded to darken Abigail's eyelashes. 'A little dusting of rouge and you are done to a turn,' cried Hannah.

Oh, the wonder of clothes! Abigail felt like a new and alluring woman. Her eyes were shining with excitement.

'The dinner-bell,' said Hannah in dismay.

She and Deborah rushed off. Deborah was already dressed for dinner in a rose silk gown, a necklace of garnets, and a gold-and-garnet tiara—garnets being the latest vogue—but she wanted to study her reflection and add extra perfume, and Hannah had not even changed.

In the drawing-room before dinner, it became clear that Mrs Conningham was not offended by Deborah's lending her daughter a gown. Far from it. She could hear herself genteelly murmuring to her friends over the teacups, 'So sad for poor Abigail to have nothing really proper to wear, but her friend, Lady Deborah, who is monstrous fond of her, rushed to the rescue.'

Hannah made sure that she held all Mrs Conningham's attention to keep that lady away from the captain.

She was too busy enjoying the effect Abigail's appearance was having on the captain to notice that the Earl of Ashton was taken aback by the picture Deborah made.

The rose silk gown flattered Deborah's excellent figure and showed the whiteness of her bosom. As was the current fashion, she carried one end of the skirt looped over her arm to show one excellently shaped leg. Deborah had muttered to her surprised brother that he must appear to make something of a play for Abigail but without interfering in that young lady's conversation with Captain Beltravers, and so Abigail found herself being flattered by the handsome Lord William and appeared almost as pretty as she thought she now looked.

They all sat down to dinner in high spirits. The captain was once more thinking seriously of asking Abigail to wed him; Abigail was glowing with an infectious happiness; Mrs Conningham was in high alt to be so surrounded by titles; Hannah was proud of her success as lady's-maid; Deborah was enjoying the occasional flash of admiration she caught in the earl's eyes when he looked at her; William was thinking of Clarissa and wondering how soon he could get to London; and the earl was pleased that the twins should show themselves to be such a goodlooking, pleasant pair.

All was going as merry as a marriage bell until the earl turned to order more wine, caught the eye of one of his elderly footmen, and the footman crossed his fingers to ward off the evil eye.

'What do you mean by that?' roared the earl. 'Judd,' he said to his butler, 'what does James mean? Has he gone mad?'

The butler approached his master, trembling. 'It's said the devil is in this house, my lord,' he quavered.

'What superstitious rubbish is this?' demanded the earl.

'It was Lady Carsey. She came here this afternoon, my lord, and she saw something which unhinged her mind. While she was waiting for her carriage, she was weeping and praying and making the sign of the cross.'

'Lady Carsey?'

'I think that has something to do with me and Benjamin,' said Hannah. 'I sent him up that tree outside the drawing-room windows to get a cat down—it turned out to be one of the stable cat's kittens. Lady Carsey was looking out. She must have seen Benjamin's face looming up out of the mist and her conscience must have smitten her at last, for she did try to have him hanged.'

William began to laugh and laugh. In desperation, Deborah tried to signal to him to be quiet, but he paid her no heed.

'You know something about this, Lord William,' said the earl, his green eyes narrowing. 'Out with it!'

'She *did* send someone to kill Miss Pym and Benjamin,' said William, mopping his eyes. 'Deb and I went on the stage-coach masquerading as Miss Pym and Benjamin. Lady Carsey sent some creature called Fotheringay to put poison in our coffee. Deb caught him in the act and switched the cups. God, was that fellow ill. I found him in the necessary house, puking up his guts.' William burst out laughing again while the rest looked at him in horror.

'Well, don't you know, I didn't want any scandal,' said William, 'and he had got rid of the poison and it would only be our word against his, and then, Ashton, you turned up to take us home.'

'Yes, go on,' said the earl grimly, remembering how strangely meek and biddable the twins had been.

'There's better,' crowed William. 'We thought, why should this Lady Carsey get off scot-free, so Deb and I decided to *haunt* her. We dressed up in our disguises and crept into her bedchamber at old Langford's and gave her the fright of her life. You should have heard her scream when I lit that magnesium powder! Like a hundred cats with their tales in the mangle. Don't you see the prime joke? It was misty this afternoon, and when she looked out, she must ha' thought Miss Pym and Benjamin had come up from the grave to get her!'

And William leaned back in his chair and laughed and laughed.

The earl waited in stony silence until he had finished. Then he said coldly to his butler, 'And why is it that *I*, who had nothing to do with this, am supposed to have the evil eye?'

The butler miserably shuffled his feet. 'The servants say so, my lord, as how you look like the devil since you came back from the wars.'

There was a long silence. William had caught his sister's horrified look and had stopped laughing. Both he and Deborah were suddenly thinking the same thing. The furious earl would write to their father now.

And then there came a snort of laughter. The Earl of Ashton was actually laughing. He was leaning back in his chair and roaring with laughter. Everyone else began to laugh as well out of sheer relief.

'Be off with you, Judd,' said the earl when he could, 'and take that clown, James, with you. I will talk to all the servants later.' He smiled at Deborah. 'You have saved me a journey, for I fully meant to travel to Esher to warn Lady Carsey never to approach Miss Pym or Benjamin again. But Fotheringay is not a hired thug, he is an effeminate fop and her nephew. One day he will cross my path and then he will be sorry. But you ridiculous pair, you could have been killed!'

Deborah flushed and looked miserable, Hannah noticed. The earl was once more looking at the twins as if they were reprehensible scamps. 'I think she wants *him!*' thought Hannah, her matchmaking mind racing. 'I must do something.'

Hannah was so absorbed in this new problem that she forgot to keep a close watch on Mrs Conningham and realized too late, when they were all gathered again in the drawing-room, that that lady had trapped the captain in a corner and was talking animatedly. There is nothing worse, nothing more terrifying, thought Hannah, than a widow woman of small means with marriageable daughters. The captain's smile was becoming fixed.

'Do play us something, Miss Conningham,' urged Hannah, hoping that the captain would walk to the piano to turn the music. But it was Lord William who stood beside Abigail.

'Lady Deborah,' begged Hannah, 'do go and get that woman away from the captain, please.'

The earl curiously watched all this by-play. He saw Deborah sail up to Mrs Conningham and say something and then both she and Mrs Conningham retired to a corner. Then Hannah went over to the piano and murmured something to William, who looked up with a start, nodded, and walked over to the fireplace.

'Why, Captain Beltravers,' said Hannah, 'I do believe Miss Conningham has been left neglected.' He gave her a half-bow and went over to the piano to turn the sheets of music.

Hannah next bore down on Mrs Conningham and Deborah, waving a piece of needlework she had extracted from her large reticule and begging Mrs Conningham to examine the laying of the stitches—'But the light is poor here. We would be better over by the candelabrum.'

That left Deborah alone. The earl politely joined her, shooting a suspicious glance at Hannah Pym, and wondering if that was what she meant to happen.

'All sorts of undercurrents, Lady Deborah,' he said. 'Am I wrong, or does our indefatigable Miss Pym mean to try to make a match between Miss Conningham and the captain?'

'If she does, I think she will prove to have a lighter hand than poor Miss Conningham's mama,' said Deborah.

'And Miss Conningham is wearing a very modish gown. Five hundred guineas at least, by my reckoning. It would not be one of yours, by any chance?'

Deborah bit her lip and then said, 'And why

not? Her own gowns are sadly dashed.'

'True. But it fascinates me to see you aiding and abetting Miss Pym's machinations. I would have said you had not one streak of femininity in your whole body.'

That hurt. Deborah felt a stabbing pain. Was she not wearing one of her best gowns, one she had never worn before? She forgot that it was her father who had ordered her wardrobe and that she normally preferred to wear men's clothes. All she could think of was that before she came down, her glass had told her she was looking very pretty and that now she felt like a drab.

'You must not go by outside appearances, my lord,' she said quietly.

'I was not going by outside appearances. At this moment, you look one of the most beautiful and delectable ladies I have ever seen,' said the earl lightly. 'I was referring to your hoydenish behaviour.' Deborah really only heard that he had called her beautiful and glowed with an inner light which lent such a radiance to her golden hair and blue eyes that the earl caught his breath.

Over at the piano, the captain had just said he felt tired and thought he would turn in early, and in Abigail's soul all the lights went out, leaving her sitting on the piano stool, a young lady of no particular charm or looks whatsoever. One curl unwound itself from the perfect arrangement on her head and drooped down to her shoulder, as if her very hair were straightening in sympathy with her mood.

William stood moodily by the fireplace, wondering what to do. The evening had turned curst flat and there was Deb behaving like a flirt. The earl was saying something and Deb had a pink colour on her cheeks and was lowering those long eyelashes of hers and waving her fan slowly to and fro. Now it was William who felt the end of the closeness he had shared with his sister and resented it. He did not stop to think it odd that he himself had been captured by such feminine behavior from Clarissa. He only knew he wanted to put a stop to it. Ashton was old enough to be Deb's father, he thought, becoming furious. He went over and stood in front of them.

'What about taking a rod out tomorrow, Deb?' he asked, ignoring the earl.

She blinked up at him as if coming back from a long way away.

'I do not think so, William. Miss Pym and the others will be here tomorrow. It would be pleasant to spend a little time with them.'

'Pooh, if you want to waste your time with a redcoat who has little to say for himself, and a dowdy matron and her tiresome daughter, you can do it without me.'

'Don't be so rude!' flashed Deborah.

But the earl put a hand on her arm and said quietly, 'You surprise me, William, as no doubt Miss Clarissa Carruthers will be surprised.'

'What do you mean, sir?' asked William.

'Why, only that I am going to finish writing a letter to Mr Carruthers and his sister on the morrow. I promised to let them know how the coach party got on. Miss Carruthers was much taken with Miss Pym and her stories.'

'As I am,' put in William quickly.

'And Miss Abigail Conningham. Miss Carruthers thought her such a sweet girl.'

'Demme, if I don't think the same,' said William, tugging at his shirt collar.

'But you said. . .'

'Talking nonsense. Bit liverish.'

'And you so young,' mocked the earl. 'Shall I give Miss Carruthers your wishes when I write?'

'Of course, please do.'

'I am glad she still holds your interest. I was beginning to think you were paying court to Miss Conningham.'

'Oh, that was Miss Pym's matchmaking plans,' said William quickly. 'Get the captain to show an interest.'

'How worthy of you.' The earl turned to Deborah. There was now a warm caressing note in his voice that William did not like. 'Why trouble to travel back to Downs Abbey tonight? I can send the servants over to collect your night-things. Stay here.'

'Thank you,' said Deborah and lowered those ridiculously long eyelashes of hers again.

But William felt he could not protest. The earl was writing to Clarissa, and that report must be favourable. But he did not want to lose the boyish Deb, his sister, and see her permanently become this strange new creature who flirted and who moved with a new sinuous grace as if suddenly aware of her own body for the first time.

He moved away and then an idea hit him and he muttered excuses and left the room. He would have been relieved had he stayed to listen to the conversation between the earl and his sister. The earl, encouraged by Deborah, had started to talk of all that needed to be done to the house and estate, and as Deborah took a great interest in the running of her father's estates, she was able to offer sensible advice. Surprised, and gratified, the earl talked on, and while he talked, Deborah thought rather bleakly that he was talking to her as if she were a man. No more pretty compliments.

When the party broke up and went upstairs, Hannah waited until she was sure Mrs Conningham would have gone to bed and went to Abigail's room. That young lady was sitting, still dressed, on the end of the bed, staring into space.

'It is not going to work,' said Abigail when she saw Hannah.

'You must not be cast into despair the whole time,' said Hannah bracingly. 'You have another day and then the whole rest of the journey to Dover. How would it be if I arranged with the earl that Benjamin take myself and your mother out for a drive tomorrow afternoon? You would be left alone with your captain.'

Hope shone again in Abigail's eyes. 'Could you do that?'

'I think so,' said Hannah. 'Only leave it to me.'

*　　　*　　　*

In his bedchamber, the earl climbed into bed and stretched out his long legs. Then he leaped up with a cry and jerked back the sheets. Stuffed down at the end of his bed was a gorse bush.

Fuming, he took a pair of tweezers out of his manicure set and removed several gorse prickles from the soles of his feet. He was bitterly disappointed in Deborah. She had seemed such a mature and attractive lady when he had been talking to her about his estates and the need for improvement.

In her room, Deborah, in night-dress and lacy wrapper, looked miserably at her short golden curls in the glass. Men like the earl no doubt thought hair a woman's crowning glory. Not that she was in love with him or anything stupid like that. It was just, oh, it was just mortifying that her kiss had seemed to have so little effect on him. Now if her hair were longer. . . She shrugged her shoulders and decided to read herself to sleep and forget about the earl. There was a small pile of books considered suitable for a lady on an occasional table. She picked them up. *Five Hundred Embroidery Stitches,* by 'a Lady'; *The Perils of Lady Marcheson or The Wicked Italian Count* by Mrs Bradford; Mr Porteous's *Sermons*; The Holy Bible; and *Putnam's Formulas for Beauty.*

She seized on the last and turned the pages eagerly. 'Hair, hair, hair,' she mumbled. 'Ah, here it is. Nothing for lengthening hair. But straightening hair . . . yes, that might do the trick.'

Like all people with very curly hair, Deborah often longed for straight hair. Hannah Pym might have pointed out to her that any young lady who has not endured the hell of sleeping in curl papers or clay rollers longs for straight hair, something which seems quite mad to most of the rest of her sex. But Deborah became convinced that straight hair would mean longer hair. She eagerly read the recipe. Half a pound of petrolatum, half a pound of rendered mutton suet, three ounces of beeswax, two ounces of castor oil, ten grains of benzoic acid, one fluid dram of lemon grass and fifteen drops of cassia oil.

She could not wait. Between the kitchen and the still-room, she could put together the ingredients, and the kitchen fire, with luck, might still be alight, as the mixture would need to be heated.

She crept silently downstairs, or as silently as she could, for the wooden treads on the great staircase creaked abominably.

In his bedchamber, the earl, still awake, heard that tell-tale creaking. He was all at once sure it was the twins up to more mischief.

He got out of bed, after lying awake for fifteen minutes and wondering whether he should leave them to their own devices, pulled on a rich embroidered dressing-gown, picked up his bed-candle and made his way out. He went down to the hall and raised his candle high and looked around. Then he saw that the green baize door to the kitchens was standing open.

He walked down the stone steps of the back stairs. The servants' hall was deserted, but there was a light shining under the kitchen door.

He softly opened the kitchen door.

Deborah was standing there, looking down at an assortment of items spread out on the scrubbed deal table. 'What are you doing?' he asked sharply.

Deborah jumped guiltily. 'I was hungry and. . . and . . . came down to see if there was anything to eat.'

He walked forward and looked down at the assortment on the table. 'Beeswax,' he murmured. 'Benzoic acid . . . are you trying to create another terrible practical joke?'

Deborah hung her head.

'I thought this evening you had finally grown up, Lady Deborah,' said the earl heavily. 'That was until I found the gorse bush which you and your brother had placed in my bed.'

'That was nothing to do with me!' cried Deborah. 'Oh, William, I could *kill* you. That must have been why he was out of the drawing-room for so long. I noticed his pumps were muddy when he came back.'

'Well, well, let us say you are blameless. You had better tell me what you are doing with such an odd assortment.'

Deborah turned fiery red. 'I was trying to straighten my hair.' She pushed forward a small book. 'I found a recipe for a hair straightener in here.'

The earl's green eyes began to dance. 'Why destroy your golden curls?'

Deborah ran her fingers through them and sighed. 'My hair is so very short.'

'Come, let us put all this stuff away. Your curls will be the envy of all the ladies when you go to London.'

'Why should I go to London?'

'For the same reason most young ladies go to London—to make a come-out and find a husband.'

'I do not need to find a husband,' said Deborah. 'Papa has money enough.'

'What a condemnation of the state of matrimony.'

'It is *true*. Only look at poor Miss Abigail, condemned to marry an old man because of his money, or rather because of her uncle's money, for he is to help the family if she does as she is bid.'

'If Miss Pym has her way, then she will have her captain. Perhaps I should engage the services of Miss Pym to find me a bride,' said the earl.

'You?' Deborah looked shaken. 'You are a bachelor.'

'I could not marry before this. I had nothing to offer a wife. I was in the army.'

'That did not stop Captain Beltravers having a wife.'

'Only look what became of the poor woman. My father kept me on short commons, so I doubted very much if I could support a family before this inheritance.' The earl eyed her thoughtfully. 'Yes, I should definitely discuss the matter with Miss Pym.'

'And what do you look for in a bride?' asked Deborah.

'Grace and manner and wit and kindness. Looks are not important, nor the length of her hair.'

Deborah began to pick up bottles and jars. 'Then ask Miss Pym tomorrow,' she said tartly.

He took some bottles from her and they walked through to the still-room and Deborah began to put everything away, letting out an involuntary shiver, for the room was cold.

149

'Come, that's enough,' he said. 'The servants can clear the rest away in the morning. Back to bed with you.'

Deborah was suddenly very conscious of the nearness of him in the small still-room, of the faint scent of cologne he wore. She said breathlessly, 'Yes, yes. I am a little tired.'

'Then come along.' They walked back up to the hall together.

'Are you very angry with William?' asked Deborah.

'I'll teach the young fool a lesson before I go to bed. He should have grown out of such tricks. I am glad you had nothing to do with it.'

'You believe me?' said Deborah in a small voice.

He ruffled her curls and smiled down at her indulgently as they stood together in the hall. 'Yes, my chuck.'

'Do not do that!' said Deborah sharply, backing away. 'I am a woman, not a child.'

'Yes,' he said softly. 'Yes, I had noticed. You looked very beautiful this evening—you are very beautiful and will break many hearts.'

Deborah gulped. 'I d-don't want to break h-hearts.'

He put his candle down on a table and put a long finger under her chin and tilted it up. 'I should write to your father,' he said softly, 'and warn him of the enchantress his daughter has become.' He stooped and kissed her gently on the mouth, startled to receive the same dizzying shock he had experienced when he kissed her before. He wrapped his arms around her and kissed her deeper.

William, above them on the landing, looked down in horror at the couple in each other's arms, standing in the pool of light shed by the candle. He had gone in search of Deborah to tell her about his prime joke on the earl, confident that such a mild practical joke would not prompt the earl to damn him with Clarissa.

He now forgot about Clarissa. Deborah was leaving him for that adult world of conventions and marriage. Gone were all the easy days of companionship, of hunting and fishing.

Whatever it was between Ashton and his sister must be stopped. He crept away. If he interrupted them, demanded that Ashton state his intentions, then he was dismally sure that Puritan Ashton would promptly point out that his intentions were honourable. He must think up some way to stop him.

The earl released Deborah and said, 'You are trembling.'

'So are you,' said Deborah shakily.

'It is cold and we are behaving quite disgracefully. What would Miss Pym say?' He dropped a light kiss on her nose and picked up the candle. 'I shall see you tomorrow,' he said huskily. 'There is much we have to discuss.'

Deborah felt dizzy and light-headed. She was sure he loved her. He would not have kissed her otherwise, not Puritan Ashton.

Outside her door, she gave him a shy good night.

William was lying in bed, pretending to be asleep as he heard the door of his room open. No doubt Ashton had arrived to read the riot act. The earl went quietly over to the toilet-table and picked up a full jug of water. He walked over to the bed and tipped the contents over William's head. William sat up spluttering. From the darkness came the earl's mocking voice, 'Do not ever play tricks on me again, young William, or it will be the worse for you.' Then William heard the door close.

He sat up in bed, cursing, and fumbled with his tinder-box until he was able to light the bed-candle. He got up and dried himself and put on his clothes and sat sulkily in a chair by the fire. Damn Ashton. There must be some way to pay him out and keep Deb free of him.

And then he remembered Ashton had said something about writing to Clarissa and her brother. A great idea struck him. If he could find that letter. . .

He went downstairs and made his way to the earl's study. There were various bills and estate books on the desk, but there on top was a half-finished letter. He drew his candle close and began to read. The earl had given the Carruthers an account of Miss Pym's further adventures and the haunting of Lady Carsey.

He put down the letter which fortunately,

he noticed, although unfinished, stopped at the end of a page. The earl obviously meant to write more before he sent it off. William took a fresh piece of paper. The earl wrote in a clear italic script, easy to copy. 'As far as Lady Deborah is concerned,' William wrote, 'she has proved quite charming out of her men's clothes and will provide me with an interesting bit of dalliance before I decide to settle on the business of finding me a wife. Perhaps you know of some suitable lady?'

William then took the two pages of the earl's letter and the page on which he had written the forgery and darted quickly up the stairs again and found his way to his sister's bedchamber.

She was lying asleep and he shook her roughly by the shoulder. 'Who is it?' demanded Deborah crossly.

'It is I, William. Wake up. You should read this.'

'Read *what?* Oh, William, I had just got to sleep. And I am so very angry with you. Whatever possessed you to play such a childish trick on Ashton?'

Her brother lit a branch of candles and carried it over to the bed. 'I was ferreting around downstairs looking for something to read and I came across this half-written letter. It's from Ashton to that Carruthers chap; you remember he said he was writing to Clarissa and her brother?'

Deborah struggled up, aghast. 'William, you have no right to read anyone else's correspondence.'

'And nor would I have,' said William righteously, 'if I had not just glanced down at it and seen your name. You need not read all, just the last page. There's only one paragraph, the letter is not finished, but it is just as well. You will find what he has written about you is bad enough.'

As Deborah read it and turned white, William felt a stab of conscience but persuaded himself fiercely he was doing it all for his sister's own good. Ashton was too old for her, and she should not be thinking of marriage yet.

'Take it away,' said Deborah, holding it out with the tips of her fingers after she had read it. She lay down and turned her face into the pillow.

'You had to know,' said William gruffly.

'Go away.'

'Don't take it so hard, Deb. Let's get out of here. I can rouse the groom and get the carriage brought round. You'll feel better at home.'

There was a long silence. He was almost on the point of saying he had forged that part of the letter when she suddenly sat up, two spots of anger burning on her white cheeks.

'Yes, William,' she said fiercely. 'Let's go home.'

154

'Good girl. Get ready and meet me outside. Don't bother to pack anything. We can send the servants for it later.'

He ran downstairs and put the earl's part of the letter back where he had found it. Then he went back to his room. The fire was nearly out, but he thrust his forgery through the bars of the grate and then went back down again, unbolted the heavy front door and ran to the mews to rouse their groom.

Twice on the road home, he nearly told his sister the truth, she was so quiet and sad. But tomorrow would surely see her restored to her old self and her old clothes and her old way of speech. In the short space of time since the earl had kissed her, she had not sworn or spoken like a groom.

Deborah felt quite cold and empty. She would never marry now. She would hunt and fish with William and they would grow old together, two eccentrics, two Originals, while the earl went to London and found himself a lady who would faint at the very sight of a female in men's clothes.

*   *   *

The earl did not discover the absence of the twins until late in the afternoon. He had had an early breakfast with Miss Pym, who, he was amused to see, seemed to have taken over the running of his household, giving orders to the

155

butler about the proper cleaning of the rooms. Then he had ridden out to visit his tenant farmers. He was looking forward to getting the work of the day over quickly so that he could tell Lady Deborah all about it. He was conscious of a happiness he had never known before.

Hannah had successfully borne Mrs Conningham off, with Benjamin driving them in a gig, which left Abigail alone with the captain, or so Hannah thought. But the captain had, just before she had left, promptly taken a horse from the stables and had ridden over to Travers's place for a further look. He did not know Hannah's plans and was glad to escape from the gushing Mrs Conningham, so Abigail was left alone with the servants to pass the time in gloomy thoughts.

The earl returned at the same time as Hannah and Mrs Conningham. Hannah noticed he looked carefree and happy. He told her to tell Lady Deborah that he would be in the drawing-room as soon as he had changed out of his muddy clothes.

It was in the drawing-room that Hannah learned of the ruin of the romances. There was Abigail, sad and downcast, to say she had not seen the captain all day, and there was Judd, the butler, to tell her that Lord William and Lady Deborah had gone home in the middle of the night and had sent servants over in the afternoon to collect their clothes.

And then the earl came in, cheerfully demanding to know where Lady Deborah was and Hannah told him the news and watched in dismay as the happiness died out of his face.

It was a grim dinner. Hannah was glad they were to leave in the morning for Dover. Something awful must have happened between the earl and Lady Deborah, and as for Captain Beltravers, well, Hannah felt like shaking *him.*

Abigail asked Hannah shyly what she should do with Lady Deborah's gown and jewellery and Hannah told her to keep the lot until she heard from Lady Deborah.

The earl was glad to go to bed and get away from them all. His heart felt heavy and he felt like a fool. He must have frightened Deborah. She must have thought him a lecherous old satyr. He was too old for her. But she might at least have said goodbye. He damned the Earl of Staye. He would not go near Downs Abbey again. Let the earl look after his own children!

*　　　*　　　*

Deborah and William spent a quiet day fishing without catching anything. Deborah was muddy and cold and depressed when they returned home. For the the first time, she felt the loss of her mother acutely. And then she thought of Hannah Pym. Miss Pym would give her bracing advice. Miss Pym would know what to do.

'William,' she said casually. 'I feel blue-devilled. I would like to know the end of the story, that is, if Miss Pym succeeds in getting Abigail and the captain together. Let's go to Dover tomorrow and surprise them. I don't want to travel in another stage-coach. We could take our own travelling-carriage.'

'Don't know that I care much what happens to them,' said William gloomily, for his conscience was beginning to torment him badly. Deb had changed now for good and would not change back, whatever he did. Even going fishing, she had worn an old woollen gown and cloak, something she had never done before, always saying men's clothes were more practical. She spoke softly and sadly and had not sworn once all day, not even when the fish did not bite.

'Besides, if we wait here, Ashton will come calling, perhaps. . .'

William sat up. What if the earl did call and Deborah told him about that letter! William began to sweat at the very idea.

'Perhaps you have the right of it,' he said with false heartiness. 'But no need for an early start. We can leave at noon and still be in Dover at the same time as the coach.'

*   *   *

'That's the last of the packing,' said Hannah, slamming down the lid of her trunk, 'except for my night-rail and a few other things which I can put in in the morning. You know, Benjamin, something awful must have happened between Lord Ashton and the twins. The earl was so elated, so happy at breakfast. Quite a different man. Then when he heard they had left, he became silent and moody.'

'Mayhap Lord William talked Lady Deborah into going,' said Benjamin.

'Why would he do that?'

'When I was on duty in the drawing-room last night,' said Benjamin, 'I couldn't help noticing how Lord William was sort o' glowering at his sister when she was talking to the earl. Didn't like it a bit.'

'We should have driven over and asked them,' said Hannah impatiently. 'Look in their rooms, Benjamin, before we leave in the morning. Despite my efforts, the old servants here are very lazy and I am convinced they will do nothing to clean out the guest bedchambers until other guests are expected.'

'Very good,' said Benjamin. He cocked his head to one side and surveyed her. 'Strikes me you would be better thinking about making a match for yourself than bothering about all these other people.'

'Benjamin!'

'Garn! I got eyes in me 'ead. It's Sir George, ain't it?'

159

'Get out of here, you impertinent jackanapes, before I throw something at your head!'

Benjamin went out grinning. Hannah sat down on the trunk. Now that she was far away from him, the very idea of a romance between such as herself and Sir George seemed totally ridiculous. Better to forget about him. Well, maybe she would see him just once more and then forget about him. Just one other outing. Just one more opportunity to see those blue eyes.

At five in the morning, the stage-coach passengers were roused and told to make ready for their journey to the Crown at Rochester to meet the coach. Benjamin suddenly remembered he had not searched the rooms. As Hannah had guessed, they had not been touched. There was no clue to anything in Lady Deborah's room. In William's, however, he looked thoughtfully down at the bed, which was still wet. That was odd. The very pillow was soaking. He looked about him. The grate was still full of cold ashes. And then Benjamin saw a spool of blackened paper sticking out between the bars in the grate.

He pulled it out and put it in his pocket just as he heard Hannah calling for him.

Despite the earliness of the hour, the earl was there to see them all off. He still looked sad and grim, thought Hannah.

In fact, what a sad lot they all were, she

reflected wearily as they all climbed aboard the stage. Abigail's eyes were red and puffed again, the captain was withdrawn and silent, and Mrs Conningham, who had finally been snubbed by the captain, was looking very down indeed.

They breakfasted at Sittingbourne, and Hannah asked if a Mr Fothgeringay was still resident but was told that they did not know anyone of that name. She described Mr Fotheringay as an effeminate-looking man who had been taken ill and was told that was a Mr Crank who had departed the day before. So Hannah was left to enjoy what she could of a quite dreadful breakfast.

As she rose to leave, Benjamin remembered the spill of paper. 'I searched those bedchambers,' he said, 'but couldn't find nuffink except it looked as if someone had poured a jug o' water over Lord William and this was stuck in the fire.'

Hannah unrolled the paper and read it, her eyebrows shooting up to her sandy hair. Deaf to the cries of 'Coach! Coach!' she sat down abruptly and smoothed out the paper and read it again.

Had this been written by the earl to someone? And had William found it and shown it to his sister? That would explain their middle-of-the-night leave-taking. But surely Ashton would never write this. Might think it, for all Hannah knew. But he would never put such words about the daughter of one of his friends and neighbours to paper.

'God help me. I hope I am doing the right thing,' said Hannah aloud. 'Benjamin,' she said, fishing in that huge reticule, 'take this money, take all you need and hire a pochay and get back to Ashton Park this day and give that to Lord Ashton and tell him where you found it. If he has written it, he will merely thank you for it. If he did not, and Lord William was trying to trick his sister, then he may deal with it as he sees fit.'

'But what is it?' asked Benjamin. 'I didn't read it.'

'Never mind,' said Hannah. 'Go like the wind!'

7

I can trace my ancestry back to a protoplasmal primordial atomic globule. Consequently, my family pride is something inconceivable. I can't help it. I was born sneering.

W.S. Gilbert

By the time the Dover coach reached its destination and rolled into the yard of the Royal George, Hannah felt she was travelling with a party of strangers. Mrs Conningham had taken against the captain and was once more obviously looking forward to getting her daughter settled in marriage with Mr Clegg. Captain Beltravers was like a soldier carved out of wood, so still and set was his face, and poor Abigail seemed resigned to her fate. All were silent.

Only Hannah and Benjamin were to put up at the inn. The Conninghams were going straight to Uncle and the captain to his regiment to resign.

Like all inns in Dover, the Royal George was very well appointed and very expensive. Few stage-coach passengers could ever afford to stay there, the majority of passengers coming to town travelling in their own carriages or by hired post-chaise.

It was Abigail who made a desperate last stand to change her future. As Hannah and the captain were murmuring their goodbyes, she said, 'But you must come with us to meet Uncle Henry, Miss Pym, and Captain Beltravers, too. We are all in need of supper and . . . and . . . Dover inns are so very expensive.'

With a surprised feeling of relief Hannah saw the captain bow and heard him say he would be delighted. Quickly she accepted herself. Mrs Conning-ham bridled and glared at her daughter, but then recollected that it would be pleasant to be accompanied by the majestic Miss Pym. In truth, she was afraid of her brother-in-law.

The evening was pale gold, gold light bathing the heaving sea and gilding the cobbles of the old town. Bad weather was coming, and up on the cliffs, black clouds were massed behind the castle. The streets were full of a mixture of fishermen, sailors, soldiers and the Quality, and a man with a telescope on the waterfront, trying to charge anyone who was interested a shilling 'to look at Napoleon'. It was generally believed that the First Consul spent his time across at Boulogne, studying the English town he soon hoped to invade.

The lamplighters were going about their work as the sun sank lower in the west and the little party made their way up the narrow, winding, fish-smelling streets under the wheeling, crying seagulls to Uncle Henry's house, a great square building above the town. It fronted onto the street, without a garden, its name, The Crow's Nest, being chiselled into the brickwork.

Benjamin rang a ship's bell outside the door, which was opened by a smart maid in a ribboned cap and muslin apron.

'Mr Conningham has been expecting you this age, mem,' she said to Mrs Conningham, and then led the way up a narrow flight of polished wooden stairs to the drawing-room, which was on the first floor.

It was a long narrow room with mullioned windows and beechwood panelling. The low ceiling was beamed and had oil-lamps hanging from it, and the whole had more the air of a captain's cabin than a drawing-room.

Uncle Henry walked forward to meet them, listening gravely to Mrs Conningham's breathless introductions. He was a puffy, wheezy, sententious man who had compressed his circumference into a very tight blue coat with buttons the size of tart plates. He was wearing buff breeches, also very tight, and gauze stockings through which the hairs of his legs bristled angrily. He had bulbous staring eyes, which gave him the appearance of always being in a temper. But he unbent graciously when Hannah took her seat with Benjamin behind her, and remarked that Clara, Mrs Conningham, was indeed fortunate to have travelled in such distinguished company. He himself would never travel by stage-coach. 'The Conninghams came over with the Normans,' he said. 'That is why we have the Nose. We are a proud family.' He turned his profile to Hannah, exhibiting a rather fat pockmarked nose and Hannah found it hard not to laugh.

A man who had been sitting in a shadowy part of the room came forward and made his bow. 'Mr Clegg,' said Mr Conningham.

Hannah looked at Abigail's dismal face. Mr Clegg was grey-haired. The miniature he had sent had been of himself as a younger man. He had watery green eyes and sharp features.

Wine was served all round and then there

was an awkward silence. Mrs Conningham, who had been looking forward to bragging about her stay at the earl's, found now that she could not open her mouth. Ever optimistic, she had hoped that Mr Clegg would prove to be superior to his miniature, but he had proved inferior and already her tired mind was running through household budgets, wondering how they would now manage, for she knew at least she could not constrain Abigail to marry such a creature. She threw one hurt and wounded look at the captain. He could have solved the whole problem.

'So,' said Uncle Henry, 'we will go in to dine as soon as Jane is with us.'

'Jane!' cried Mrs Conningham. 'What is *she* doing here?'

'Why, some kind lady—why, I believe it was Miss Pym here—sent her her fare and told her she was needed in Dover.'

'Miss Pym!' exclaimed Mrs Conningham, high colour on her cheeks. 'How dare you!'

Before Hannah could reply, Mr Clegg stood up and hitched his thumbs in his buttonholes and said, 'You must not be angry, Mrs Conningham. What I have to say will warm your maternal heart. I beg leave to pay my addresses to Miss Jane. She has captured my heart.'

'Well, my, goodness, what am I to say, sir?' said poor Mrs Conningham. 'You, sir, were promised to Abigail.'

'Tush,' said Uncle Henry. He turned to Hannah. 'You did well, ma'am, to send such a priceless pearl to my friend, Mr Clegg. What comparison can there be between Abigail and Jane, I ask you? Jane has the Norman features of a true Conningham. We are a proud name, Miss Pym, a proud name.'

The door opened and Jane came into the room. Hardly a beauty, thought Hannah, but much as I expected. Jane Conningham had large, rather full brown eyes and great brown sausage curls on her head. Her plump figure was poured into a slip of white muslin. She was all dimples: dimpled cheeks, dimpled elbows—and dimpled who knows where else, thought Hannah sourly.

'Jane, is this true?' asked Mrs Conningham. 'Do you wish to marry Mr Clegg?'

'Oh, yes, Mama,' said Jane, flashing a look of pure malice at her sister.

'Then I suppose,' said Mrs Conningham faintly, 'that I must give you my permission, Mr Clegg.'

He took Jane's plump hand in his. 'You have made me the happiest of men,' he said, and Jane giggled and blushed and looked triumphant.

When they filed in for dinner, Hannah took the opportunity to mutter to Abigail, 'Do not ever let your sister know you are relieved or she might change her mind.'

Happy at last, Mrs Conningham began to tell of their stay at the Earl of Ashton's home. She could not have hit on a better subject. Uncle Henry obviously got a great amount of vicarious pleasure out of the story. 'We Conninghams only consort with the best,' he said.

Hannah was seated next to Captain Beltravers at dinner. 'And what are your plans now?' asked Hannah.

'I shall go to my regiment and start arrangements to sell out.'

'And then?'

He smiled suddenly. 'Why, then I shall take up residence in three months' time in Travers's place.'

'You *bought* it?'

'Indeed yes, Miss Pym, and the earl was right, a good bargain it is, too.'

Hannah felt like shaking him. Could he not have told Abigail? Abigail who had been so kind to him. Damn the man. She, Hannah Pym, was a failure as a matchmaker. She did not count Jane. The old housekeeper Hannah would have been amazed—for she considered herself a very hard-headed practical woman—if anyone had told her that, in the future, anything other than a love match was considered a failure by Miss Hannah Pym.

She turned to Uncle Henry on her other side and by way of a sort of self-flagellation asked him to tell her all about the ancestry of the Conninghams. The conceited old buffoon did just that until, behind Hannah, Benjamin stifled a yawn and Hannah herself thought she would die of boredom.

At least the tedious meal was over. Hannah said she had to leave immediately, she was fatigued after the journey, and the captain made his farewells as well. Although he kissed Abigail's hand, he said nothing about seeing her again and Hannah's soft heart was wrung by the disappointment and distress in the girl's eyes.

They made their way out and back down the narrow twisted street under the flickering lamps. 'Thank goodness, that's over,' said Hannah.

'Pompous old windbag,' commented Benjamin from behind her. For once, Hannah did not chide him.

'Not a very pleasant set of future in-laws, I'll grant you,' said the captain.

Hannah seized his arm and stopped him. 'What did you say?' she demanded shrilly.

The captain looked surprised. 'I said they were not a very pleasant set of future in-laws,' he repeated. 'But I shall make sure their visits are brief and few and far between.'

'Do you mean you are going to ask Miss Abigail to wed you?' screamed Hannah.

The captain backed away. 'Ma'am, I thought that was obvious.'

Exasperated, Hannah seized the startled captain and shook him so hard that his long pigtail bounced against his back.

'No . . . it . . . is . . . not . . . obvious,' said Hannah between shakes. She let him go and looked at him in disgust. 'There is poor Abigail, all set for a dismal night crying her eyes out because she thinks you have forgot her already. Go back there, sir. Go back there this minute and put her out of her misery, or I, Hannah Pym, will hit you with this umbrella until I beat some sense into your thick head.'

She raised her trusty umbrella threateningly and the captain backed farther away.

'But this evening was not the time, Miss Pym,' pleaded the captain. 'She had just arrived. . . and. . .'

'Benjamin!' ordered Hannah. 'Get his arm.'

The footman seized the captain in a strong grip and Hannah took his other arm. 'Now, *march!*' she ordered.

Abigail was sitting silently in the drawing-room while her uncle pontificated on about the glory of the Conninghams and her mother listened as if she were enchanted with every word and sister Jane flirted with Mr Clegg and kept flashing triumphant glances across the room.

'It was such a pity I could not get our Abigail settled too,' said Mrs Conningham when Uncle Henry paused for breath. 'Captain Beltravers is a very warm man and was set on buying a large property near the earl, but he turned out to be most rude.'

'He was not rude at all,' said Abigail shakily.

'Poor Abby,' said Jane with a laugh. 'Is that why you are so miserable? Or is it because I've got your beau?' She rapped Mr Clegg playfully with her hand and laughed again gaily.

The door opened and the smart maid called out, 'Captain Beltravers.'

Having found that the captain was a future man of property, Uncle Henry beamed a welcome. 'Did you forget anything, sir?'

'Yes, yes, I did,' said the captain hurriedly. 'Mrs Conningham, Miss Pym has persuaded me that there is after all no time like the present. I wish leave to pay my addresses to your eldest daughter, Abigail.'

There was a stunned silence. Hannah Pym should have been there to see how plain and sad Abigail became transformed into a happy, pretty young lady. Jane glared at her sister. Mr Clegg took Jane's hand and she pettishly snatched her hand away.

'You have the permission of a Conningham,' said Uncle Henry.

'Ma'am?' The captain looked at the dazed Mrs Conningham.

'Yes, of course.'

'Then may I be allowed a few moments in private with your daughter?'

'By all means.' Uncle Henry answered for her. 'Mary,' he said to the waiting maid, 'show

Miss Conningham and Captain Beltravers to the Blue Saloon.'

The grandly named Blue Saloon turned out to be no more than a small poky place full of dusty furniture. It was very cold.

'Perhaps,' said the captain when he was alone with Abigail, 'the blue comes from the colour one turns if left here too long. Abigail, will you have me?'

'Of course I will. Why did you make me so wretched? You never said anything.'

He laughed. 'I had it all planned out in my head, you see. I was so sure you knew.' He debated whether to say he was so disgusted by the mercenary blandishments of her mother that he had put off declaring himself, but wisely decided against it. He went on, 'Miss Pym was about to assault me in the street when she heard I meant to propose and had not.'

She looked at him shyly. 'I know I can never replace your wife and son in your affections . . .' she began.

The captain looked at her in surprise. 'But I love you,' he exclaimed, as if making a great discovery. It was a good thing Hannah Pym was not present to witness such romantic clumsiness.

But Abigail's face was glowing as she looked up at him and then stood on tiptoe to plant a shy kiss on his cheek.

He caught her to him and kissed her

passionately and would have gone on kissing her all night had not Uncle Henry's loud 'ahem' from the doorway made them start apart.

'Now, now,' said Uncle Henry, waving a playful finger. 'Enough of that after you're married.'

*   *   *

Out in the street, in front of the house, Hannah shivered. 'Come along, modom,' said Benjamin. 'No need to wait.'

There was a bright flash of lightning followed by a peal of thunder and then the rain came bucketing down. Hannah unfurled her umbrella and commanded Benjamin to share its shelter. 'I am going to wait here until I hear the happy ending, even if it takes all night,' said Hannah. 'Oh, if only things could work out well now for Lady Deborah.'

*   *   *

Earlier that day, Lord William had heard the rumble of carriage wheels and looked out of the window of the morning-room, which commanded a good view of the drive. With a sinking heart, he recognized the Earl of Ashton, driving his racing curricle. Then, as the earl got down, he took a piece of smoke-blackened paper out of his pocket and studied it before marching up the steps and ringing the bell.

William flew down to the hall. 'Silvers,' he hissed urgently to the butler. 'That is Ashton. You must tell him that Lady Deborah and I have gone out for a day's fishing and are not expected back until late. And warn all the other servants.'

He darted back up the stairs and hid on the landing. He could hear the earl's angry voice and Silvers's quiet one. Then, to his relief, he heard the closing of the door and the sound of the earl's driving off.

'What are you doing there?' came his sister's voice behind him, making him jump.

'I was stooping down to tie my lace,' said William. 'Noon's too late to leave, sis. Let's go now.'

'After I have breakfasted,' replied Deborah.

'I say, let's have breakfast on the Dover road.'

Deborah hesitated. The words the earl had written came back into her mind. How could she even begin to think about eating?

'Yes, let us go,' she said and William ran downstairs to order the carriage.

Soon they were off on the road and then their coachman was negotiating the press of traffic in the centre of Rochester. One of the earl's elderly footmen was creaking past. He was glad to be away from Ashton Park and out on an errand, for the earl was in a foul temper. He was like a bear with a sore head. Some said it was because his servants had had the temerity to think he was the devil incarnate, others that it was because Lady Deborah and Lord William had left in the middle of the night. The fun of believing the earl was the devil had been verbally knocked out of the servants after the earl's lecture, leaving them facing a master who constantly berated them on superstition combined with down-right laziness. The footman looked up and recognized the Earl of Staye's coachman. 'Whither bound?' he called.

'Dover,' replied the coachman, and seeing a gap in the traffic, moved on. Silvers had forgotten to tell the stable staff that Lord William and Lady Deborah were supposed to be out fishing.

The footman drove the Ashton Park gig back to the earl's home, hoping his master had recovered his humour. He was just crossing the hall when the butler told him that the earl had left for Downs Abbey in a fury, in fact worse than ever.

'Then he'll be awful when he returns,' said the footman with gloomy relish, 'for I saw 'em, Lord William and Lady Deborah, in a coach bound for Dover.'

The earl's staff crept about their duties dreading his return.

He came back in the afternoon and strode in with a face like thunder and called for brandy. 'Judd,' he said to his butler, 'tell them to change the horses and have the carriage ready, for I mean to return to Downs Abbey this night.'

'But, my lord,' quavered the butler. 'Footman Charles do say as how Lord William and Lady Deborah are on their way to Dover, for he saw their coach pass through Rochester.'

The earl swore awfully. 'I leave now,' he snapped. 'Let me know as soon as a fresh team is hitched up.'

*   *   *

Hannah Pym entered the inn with a light step. Captain Beltravers had eventually emerged to give her the good news.

She told Benjamin to have an early night, that she would see him in the morning; and she walked up to her bedchamber.

Lady Deborah, who had been sitting by the fire, rose to meet her.

'What are you doing here?' cried Hannah. 'You should be *there.*'

'I need to see you, Miss Pym,' said Deborah in a low voice. 'The most dreadful thing happened.' William, who knew his sister was waiting to see Miss Pym and had been going to join her, stopped short outside the door, listening hard. Deborah would tell Miss Pym about that letter and Miss Pym would counsel

176

her to forget about the earl and that would be an end of it. He had not thought about Clarissa recently, but now he did. He felt what he needed was to be flattered and flirted with. Perhaps after a few days in Dover, he could persuade Deborah to go to Aunt Jill's in London.

He pressed one ear harder against a panel of the door.

Deborah was telling Miss Pym about the letter.

'I know all about that,' said Hannah, and William stiffened in surprise. 'I could not understand why you both chose to leave in the middle of the night and so I sent Benjamin to search your rooms to see if there was any clue. The portion of the letter you describe, Benjamin found thrust into the fire in Lord William's room. The intention had obviously been to burn it, but it was still legible. Now let me tell you, Lady Deborah, I am convinced that Lord Ashton would never have written such words about the daughter of an old friend. Never! And why should this portion be in your brother's room? Would he stoop to forgery?'

'William? How can you say such a thing, Miss Pym?'

'Well,' said Hannah stubbornly, 'I was so convinced that it was not written by the Earl of Ashton that before we left for the inn at Rochester to join the stage, I sent Benjamin with it to the earl.'

William stood outside, biting his thumb. He knew the earl had it but had assumed he had found it in the fireplace.

He could only pray that Deb would still believe that Ashton had written it. Downstairs there was a great bustle. Some notable had arrived, for the landlord was crying, 'Show Concord'—Concord being the bedchamber assigned to the very important. 'My lord's valise and hot water to Concord. You will find a good fire of sea coal, my lord. This way, my lord. Make way for the Earl of Ashton!'

William scampered back to his room and stuffed his clothes into his trunk. He would flee to that old friend of his in Dover and demand sanctuary.

As the earl's valet unpacked his clothes, the earl rang for the waiter and asked if Lord William and Lady Deborah Western were guests at the inn, and being told they were, demanded they present themselves before him immediately. The waiter returned to say neither was in their room.

'Pym,' said the earl suddenly. 'A Miss Pym.'

'Yes, my lord. In Defiance, my lord.'

'Then tell her . . . no, show me the way.'

The waiter led the way to Defiance, the rooms being named after ships of His Majesty's navy. The earl opened the door and walked straight in.

Deborah started up at the sight of him.

'Why,' said the earl, his green eyes gleaming with a furious light, 'was this piece of filth found in your brother's room, Lady Deborah?' He shook the piece of paper at her.

'Miss Pym told me about it. In fact, William showed me the whole letter to Mr Carruthers and his sister.'

'And you believed I would write such a thing?' Hannah sidled quietly to the door, opened it and crept out.

Tears started in Lady Deborah's eyes. 'What else could I think? William told me you had written it.'

'William is going to get a horsewhipping. Why did you not simply tax me with it? Do I stand so low in your opinion?'

'I could not believe else,' whispered Deborah. 'My brother. How could I disbelieve him?'

'Just wait until I get my hands on him. Good God. Reading my private correspondence was bad enough! And as for you . . .'

He jerked her up to her feet and looked down into her blue eyes which were swimming with tears. 'Oh, Deborah,' he said thickly, 'you drive me mad.' He gathered her in his arms and began to kiss her as if he would never stop. He lifted her up and then they fell together on top of the bed and on top of Hannah Pym's chaste and virginal night-dress. 'Oh, God,' he said, caressing one soft breast, 'when are you going to marry me?'

'Whenever you want,' said Deborah. 'Kiss me again.'

Hannah Pym, waiting in the corridor, heard the bed-springs creak. One scandalized step brought her to the door. She wrenched it open and stared appalled at the spectacle of the writhing couple on the bed. She was reminded of the Duchess of Marlborough in the last century who had written proudly in her diary that the duke returning from the wars had 'pleasured' her 'in his boots' several times before breakfast. Her spinster mind could only be glad they still had all their clothes on, although the earl's hands were where no bachelor hands should be.

'Get off that bed immediately,' roared Hannah Pym.

The couple started up and laughed when they saw her, neither showing the least trace of embarrassment or shame. 'We are to be married, Miss Pym,' cried Deborah.

Hannah Pym folded her arms and glared at them. 'And so I should hope,' she said. '*So I should hope!*'

*   *   *

William's disappearance was soon discovered but no one seemed to mind. The earl, the next day, said he would take Deborah home and then write to her father and ask his permission to wed her. Hannah fervently hoped the letter and its reply would not take too long, for the passionate couple could hardly keep their hands off each other. The earl offered to take Hannah back as far as Rochester, but she primly refused. Other people's passion is very lowering to a spinster, and Hannah could only be glad when they had left.

The Royal George was very expensive indeed and so Hannah spent only one day exploring Dover before calling on Abigail in the evening to say that she and Benjamin would be taking the coach to London in the morning.

Abigail shyly pressed Hannah to attend her wedding. Hannah accepted, thinking of all the weddings she would have to attend that year.

As she sat eating a solitary dinner in the Royal George that evening, her thoughts turned to home, home and Sir George Clarence. What adventures she had to tell him! Would he come to see her as he usually did, or, horror of horrors, might he call, as he had done the time before, to say that he was engaged to be married? She was anxious to be gone. Already the characters of the stage-coach were fading from her mind. The long road to London lay before her.

The coach did not leave until ten the following morning. Hannah frowned. Should she buy Sir George a little present? It was customary for ladies to make gentlemen presents such as netted purses and things like that, but Hannah had only a few sewing items with her. Perhaps some trifle, something from Dover.

The following morning, she went out early with Benjamin to explore the little shops, shaking her head in dismay over each item. Some were too cheap and tawdry and some too expensive. At last, she settled on a ship in a bottle, a little frigate under full sail. Benjamin had fallen in love with it and urged her to buy it.

When they returned to the inn they packed and went back down to the inn yard. Captain Beltravers and Abigail were waiting for them.

'I forgot to return the gown and bracelets and headdress to Lady Deborah,' said Abigail shyly.

'I would keep them,' said Hannah, thinking in a bewildered way that Abigail and the captain were like ghosts, so firmly had she cut them from her mind in her desire to look forward now, not back. 'If Lady Deborah wants them, she will write to you. She has your address.'

Abigail laughed. 'I am to have a truly splendid wedding and Jane is furious with me. Captain Beltravers has generously offered to pay for it.'

'Is Jane regretting her engagement to Mr Clegg?' asked Hannah.

'Oh, she is pouting and flouncing and competing with me on every occasion,' said

Abigail, 'but Mr Clegg is enchanted with her and will give her everything she wants. She is persuading him to pay for a bigger wedding than mine!'

Hannah kissed her on the cheek, shook hands with the captain and then climbed aboard the coach.

Abigail and her captain stood holding hands, watching the flutter of Hannah's handkerchief at the window until they could see it no more.

'Such a fine lady,' sighed Abigail. 'I wish she could find a man worthy of her.'

'You are a romantic,' teased the captain. 'Miss Pym marry? How ridiculous!'

8

The endearing elegance of female friendship.
Samuel Johnson

Mrs Angela Courtney leaned closer to her looking glass, holding a little box of lip salve in one hand and a brush in the other. She carefully etched in a small mouth in the middle of her bigger one and then coloured it red.

She then sat back and surveyed her own reflection complacently. Her maid had recently dyed Mrs Courtney's greying hair to a rich shade of nut-brown and she was sure it took years off her. She felt a very dashing widow.

The Season, however, had been sadly flat. Mrs Courtney felt she had been a widow long enough. She kept a book with the names of eligible widowers, and one by one she had had to score them off as they succumbed to the wiles of other females or dropped dead. Her last hope, Sir Giles Cavendish, a tall thin man prone to delirium tremens and consumption, had inconveniently gone to meet his Maker the week before.

'Bring me my book, Janet,' she called to her maid, still admiring her own reflection. The maid did not need to ask, 'Which book?' Her mistress never read anything else.

Mrs Courtney ran her eyes down the now painfully short list of names. Then she saw the name of Sir George Clarence, which had a thin line scored through it. She frowned. She had scored his name out when her grapevine had told her he was on the point of proposing to a Miss Bearcroft, but that had come to nothing.

Sir George Clarence.

She carefully wrote his name in again and looked at it thoughtfully. A handsome man and a bachelor. Of course, middle-aged bachelors were notoriously difficult to catch and then the last time she had seen him he had been taking tea in Gunter's with some odd creature who looked vaguely familiar.

Mrs Courtney tapped the end of her quill

against her newly painted mouth. That woman with him. She had looked very familiar. Now where had she seen those odd eyes and that crooked nose before?

And then, all at once, she remembered.

Thornton Hall.

A housekeeper in cap and bombazine dress. That was it! Miss Pym, that had been the creature's name. And taking tea with Sir George, just as if she belonged in one of London's most fashionable establishments!

Did Sir George *know?* But then, of course he must. He was that gloomy old stick, Clarence's brother, after all. What could he be about to entertain a servant in Gunter's?

She had tried inviting Sir George to various entertainments, all of which that gentleman had refused, even a turtle dinner. People said he did not go out much in the world any more. How could she get to him?

'Janet!' she called again. 'I am going to write down the address of Sir George Clarence. I want you to go to his house and discreetly watch his comings and goings and report to me.'

'Certainly,' said the delighted Janet. The weather had turned fine and it was a great opportunity to spend time out of doors.

'What does he look like, madam?' asked Janet.

'Very distinguished. Tall and with a good profile, slim figure and very blue eyes. Elegant dresser.'

The sharp little maid enjoyed herself thoroughly out and about in the streets of London for the next few days before giving her anxious mistress her report. Sir George walked in the park at ten o'clock every morning, without fail.

Ten o'clock was a hideous early hour of the day for the fashionable Mrs Courtney, but she felt the strong lure of the chase.

There was no time to have a new walking-dress made, but she felt the best one she had would do nicely. It was of plain muslin, the front of the bodice and the sleeves being made rather full, the latter gathered with a band and finished with a bow of ribbon. On her head, on her newly brown curls, she placed a chip-straw bonnet in the cottage style with a round crown of lavender-blossom silk.

Convention made it necessary for her to take her maid, but Janet was told that once the prey was in view, she was to walk as far away as possible.

Mrs Courtney stationed herself at the gates of Hyde Park in the shadow of the high brick wall and waited. Then she saw him approaching and walked quickly into the park, only to turn about after she had gone several yards so that she might 'accidentally' meet him as he came in.

'I think I dropped my handkerchief somewhere over there,' said Mrs Courtney to her maid, just as Sir George's tall figure came into view.

'I shall go back and look, madam,' said Janet with a grin, immediately understanding the ruse.

Mrs Courtney sailed forward and then pretended to start with surprise. 'Why, Sir George!' she cooed. 'How delightful to meet you again.'

He bowed quickly to mask the frown of displeasure on his face. He enjoyed these morning walks, as he usually had the whole of the park to himself.

'Your servant, madam,' he said stiffly.

Mrs Courtney, to his irritation, wheeled about and fell into step beside him. 'Such a beautiful morning,' said Mrs Courtney. 'Ah, such sylvan rapture. I quite dote on Nature.'

'Indeed.' Sir George quickened his step, and she quickened hers accordingly.

'Now when did we last meet?' mused Mrs Courtney. She had rehearsed this, had practised an Attitude, where she would stand on one foot and playfully put one finger on the point of her chin—or where it used to be—and put her head on one side. But he was pressing on and so she practically had to run along beside him.

'Ah, I have it!' she cried. ''Twas most odd. You was entertaining some *servant* to tea in Gunter's.' Sir George stopped abruptly.

'Are your wits wandering?' he demanded

icily.

'But,' faltered Mrs Courtney, 'it was her, Miss Pym, that odd housekeeper from Thornton Hall.'

Sir George's face cleared and his eyes began to dance. 'Oh, that Miss Pym,' he said. 'Yes, she is a great friend of mine.'

'Sir George!'

'Good day to you.' He touched his hat and strode off across the park at a great rate.

He did not slacken his pace until he was sure he had left her far behind. Dreadful woman, he thought. And what harm was there in his entertaining Miss Pym if he so chose? It was not as if he were going to *marry* her.

*   *   *

Benjamin cursed Sir George under his breath. He thought Hannah was becoming dangerously overexcited. The small flat he shared with her in South Audley Street had been cleaned about ten times over to his reckoning. She was talking about buying the finest tea and the finest cakes and she had not yet had the courage to invite the man to tea.

He was used to his mistress's being calm and resolute. He did not like to see her in this dithering, anxious state.

The footman was now on his way to see Sir George Clarence. Benjamin had decided to take matters into his own hands. He had told Hannah he was tired of scrubbing and polishing and was desperately in need of fresh air. This had worked, Hannah being a great believer in the efficacy of fresh air.

Benjamin's footsteps slowed to a lagging pace as he approached Sir George's house. Perhaps it would be better to hang about and pretend to bump into him. The day was fine, but he was getting very tired of walking from one end of the street to the other when he finally saw Sir George emerge.

He strolled towards him. 'Good day, Sir George,' said Benjamin, raising a white-gloved finger to his powdered hair.

Sir George nodded and walked on, paying no more attention to Benjamin than he would have paid to any other liveried footman.

Benjamin sprinted round the streets and back again. A more direct approach was needed.

'Why, Sir George!' he cried, stopping in amazement. 'The mistress was just talking about you.'

Contrary to Mrs Courtney's now sour beliefs, Sir George did not talk to servants, nor was he used to any of the breed daring to try to strike up a conversation with him. He nodded again, swerved round Benjamin, and continued on his way. From behind him came an exasperated Cockney voice. 'Bleedin' blind old fool. I give up.'

He swung round in a fury. The liveried

footman was moodily kicking a dustbin outside an area gate.

He marched back. 'What did you say, young man?' he demanded.

'I was talking to meself, Sir George,' said Benjamin hurriedly. 'I was thinking of a character Miss Pym met on her road to Dover.'

'Why, Benjamin!' said Sir George. 'I did not recognize you. Miss Pym is returned?'

'Yes, sir, 'deed she has.'

'Well, well, I must call on her.'

Benjamin winced. Miss Pym would be thrown into a worse flutter if she had to wait for Sir George to call. The footman could gloomily imagine more scrubbing and cleaning, not to mention all the rushing to the windows at every sound of a carriage in the street.

'I would like the mistress to find larger quarters, sir,' he said earnestly. 'So cramped for entertaining, like.'

'I found Miss Pym's apartment so charming,' said Sir George, 'that I really did not notice the size of it. I would not like her to go to any trouble on my behalf. Of course, I can take her out. Tell your mistress I will call for her at three o'clock tomorrow. If that is not suitable, you may let me know. If you do not, then I shall be there at three as promised.'

'Very good, sir.' Benjamin bowed until his nose was almost touching his knee.

Sir George turned and walked away. Odd

fellow, that footman, he thought and turned and looked back in time to see Benjamin dancing down the street, occasionally performing a leap in the air and kicking his heels together.

*   *   *

Hannah listened breathlessly to Benjamin's tale of how he had happened to bump into Sir George purely by accident and of Sir George's invitation.

'Good heavens,' said Hannah. 'What an odd coincidence when you think of all the people there are in London.'

Hannah did not sleep much that night and rose at a painfully early hour, looking at the clock and reflecting that she had to live through a good few hours before three o'clock arrived.

Benjamin stayed in his room for as long as possible. He knew Hannah would be fussing and fretting and trying on one dress after the other. By noon, he was too hungry to stay in bed any longer. He rose and put on the new— or rather, new to him—livery he had bought in Monmouth Street. It had belonged to a duke's footman who had run away from his employ and had sold the livery. Benjamin had taken off the crested buttons and replaced them with plain ones. The livery was of red plush with epaulettes of gold like a field marshal's. There

191

were gold buckles at the knees and the coat was edged with gold braid. He felt he had put what was left of the prize-money after he paid his debt to good effect. He then opened a box and carefully took out a spun-glass wig and tried it on. No more powdering for him!

Hannah stared in amazement when the grandeur that was Benjamin emerged from his room.

'You do look a trifle *gaudy,*' said Hannah doubtfully.

'Me!' screeched Benjamin outraged. 'I look as fine as fivepence.'

'Yes, yes, Benjamin,' said Hannah soothingly. 'Perhaps I shall become accustomed to it. You make me look quite dowdy.'

'You've done a good enough job yourself,' said Benjamin, looking at Hannah's plain brown gown. 'What are you about, modom?'

'I look very well,' snapped Hannah. She went back into her room and stared at herself in the long mirror. The truth was that she had been trying on one gown after the other and could not make up her mind and so had settled for one of her old gowns, thinking in despair that it all did not matter anyway. He could never be interested in her.

Benjamin followed her in. 'Come now,' he said coaxingly. 'The green silk's just the thing with that pelisse to match.' He walked to the wardrobe and hooked it down. 'Does wonders for you, if I may say so, modom.'

'Are you sure?'

'Sure as eggs is eggs. Put it on.'

Sir George, arriving promptly at three, could not have guessed as he bent over the hand of the fashionably dressed lady in the green gown and pelisse what near hysteria had taken place just before his arrival, Hannah screaming that the gown was too vulgar-grand and trying to take it off, and Benjamin preventing her by tying the tapes at the back so tightly that she could not get the dress unfastened.

Hannah did not protest as the uninvited Benjamin climbed onto the back of Sir George's carriage. She felt now she needed her footman's support.

'Gunter's again, I think,' said Sir George and Hannah's soul burst out of her body, shot up into the sky like a rocket and cascaded its happy blessing over the west end of London in a shower of golden rain.

When they were seated at Gunter's, Benjamin removed himself to stand with the other footmen outside, for the famous confectioner's was too small to allow the presence of servants as well.

Hannah recounted her adventures and Sir George listened, amazed, while his untouched tea grew cold. The green dress, had Hannah but known it, had been an excellent choice, for when she was excited her odd eyes glowed green. Her hair, instead of sandy, looked the rich colour of an autumn leaf, and her sallow skin, like warm honey. She was like an interesting landscape, thought Sir George, as he watched her as she spoke: at first quite plain until you began to notice a beautiful tree and a tumbling river and the richness of the leaves on the trees.

Outside Gunter's, the other footmen regarded the vision that was Benjamin, rather like a bunch of crows finding a peacock in their midst.

'Wot you lot staring at?' demanded Benjamin angrily.

'We got the Duke o' Flummery here, boys,' jeered one. They were all idle and bored, knowing their masters and mistresses usually took a long time over their tea and confections. Baiting this newcomer seemed like excellent sport.

A tall one put his hand on his hip and began to mince up and down. 'How can we rival such magnificence?' he said.

'Stow your whids, you poxy sons o' whores,' shouted Benjamin. 'You popinjays. You with your faces like donkey's arses.'

The mincing one stopped in his tracks, his face under his white paint turning red with fury. 'There's five o' us and one o' him. Let's get 'im,' he said.

'Frightened to take me one at time?' jeered Benjamin.

They looked at him and at his deceptively tall and slight figure. 'Barney can floor you,' they said, pushing their hero forward. Barney was footman to a Mr Greystone, an effeminate, cowardly fellow who had chosen his bruiser of a footman for protection, rather than show.

'All right,' grinned Benjamin. 'Barney it is. But what's the wager?'

'You name it,' said one sulkily.

Benjamin's eyes fell on Barney's tall walking-stick, propped against one of the young plane trees which had been planted in Berkeley Square during the same year as the French Revolution, or, as the polite still called it, the Bourgeois Uprising. About five feet high, it was made of Malacca-cane, with a large silver knob on top. No footman with any aspirations to elegance should be without a walking-stick. Benjamin had longed for one, but they were very expensive and he had grown thrifty since his terrible gambling debt at Rochester, and furthermore, the second-hand-clothes shops of Monmouth Street did not run to silver-topped sticks.

'Your cane,' he said to Barney, 'if I win. Ten guineas to you if I don't.'

The footmen moved to the middle of Berkeley Square and Benjamin and Barney began to strip down to their small-clothes.

Barney's friends had never seen him stripped before and watched with some consternation as their hero removed his jacket to reveal that, under all the buckram wadding, he was a much smaller man. Then he peeled off his silk stockings and unstrapped a pair of false calves.

Two Exquisites, strolling across Berkeley Square, stopped and raised their eyeglasses. 'Servants' brawl,' said one with distaste.

The other studied Benjamin. 'Dash me!' he cried. 'Do you know who that tall thin fellow is? That's the fellow who downed Randall at Rochester.'

The word spread like lightning. Carriages quickly blocked the entries to Berkeley Square in case the tiresome militia should try to spoilsport.

'I would like some more hot tea,' said Sir George plaintively. 'Where is Gunter? Goodness, Miss Pym, little Gunter is outside his shop, watching something in the square and dancing up and down like a monkey on a stick. And where has everyone else gone?' He had been so wrapped up in Hannah's adventures that he had not noticed the confectioner's had emptied of staff and customers.

Hannah's sharp ears heard the cheering and the cries of, 'A mill! A mill!' and had a sinking feeling it all had something to do with her battling footman. Benjamin must not be allowed to disgrace her on this day of all days.

'As the shop is empty and the hot water is just over there, Sir George,' she said quickly, 'allow me to help us to more tea.'

She quickly prepared a fresh pot of tea and carried it to the table and began to elaborate on her adventures, painting such a funny picture of Mr Conningham's Norman ancestry that Sir George laughed and laughed and thought he could not remember when he had ever before been better amused.

Benjamin treated the crowd of his admirers to ten quick rounds before expertly felling Barney. He carefully put on his clothes, after making sure he had that precious stick, and then returned to his station outside Gunter's, where he lectured a large audience on the finer points of pugilism and then, feeling they should pay for his time, passed round the hat.

Gunter's filled up again, full of excited people discussing the fight. Sir George seemed deaf to it all. 'The gardens at Thornton Hall are looking magnificent, Miss Pym,' he said. 'Might I persuade you to accompany me there tomorrow?'

'I should be honoured and delighted, sir,' said Hannah demurely, while inside that green silk gown her heart tumbled and raced.

They emerged into the sunlight. There seemed to be a vast crowd. Sir George took Hannah's arm and led her to his carriage. Benjamin grabbed his new walking-stick, broke away from his audience, and strutted to Sir George's carriage and jumped on the backstrap. They were followed by a cheering crowd.

'What on earth is going on?' said Sir George, driving carefully out of Berkeley Square, not knowing the road he was on had just been unblocked. 'There must have been a raree-show. A two-headed cow or something like that. I almost thought those people were cheering us. But that is ridiculous. I do not understand society. Why must they bring the low manners of Bartholomew Fair to Berkeley Square? By Jove, one would think there had been a prize-fight.'

Hannah twisted round and flashed Benjamin a fulminating look and got a saucy wink for her pains.

Benjamin knew, when he heard the couple making arrangements to meet on the morrow, that Hannah would not give him much of a lecture. When they arrived in South Audley Street, he ran to the horses' heads as Sir George helped Hannah down.

'I just remembered,' said Sir George. 'A friend of mine was recently in York and he swore he saw Mrs Clarence walking along the street.'

'York!' exclaimed Hannah.

'So,' he said, 'if you go to York on your travels, mayhap you might find her at last.'

Hannah went slowly indoors after saying goodbye to him. Benjamin braced himself for a lecture, but Hannah simply sat down and stared into space. 'Sir George said someone saw Mrs Clarence in York, Benjamin. Do you think that can be true?'

Benjamin, anxious to avoid a row, placed his new stick tenderly in a corner by the door, and said, 'Could be. Was you thinking of travelling again, modom?'

'I don't know,' said Hannah slowly. But there was Mrs Clarence, pretty little Mrs Clarence who had run off with that footman, Mrs Clarence to whom she owed so very much. Besides, only look how enraptured Sir George had been with her tales—so enraptured that he had not even troubled to find out what was going on in the square.

'Ah, Benjamin,' said Hannah severely, 'you will now tell me how you came by that silver-topped stick, how. . . ? Stop! Where are you going?'

'Just to the booking-office,' gabbled Benjamin. 'See the price o' them tickets to York.' And he was off before Hannah could say any more.

She sat alone, brooding about Mrs Clarence and then about Sir George. That Sir George could ever look at her the way, say, that the Earl of Ashton had looked at Lady Deborah was impossible to imagine. She thought of Lady Deborah and sent up a brief prayer for her happiness before returning to worrying about Sir George.

* * *

199

Lady Deborah and the Earl of Ashton were riding neck and neck across the grounds of Downs Abbey. He eventually slowed his horse to a canter, then a trot and then to a halt and, laughing, Deborah reined in beside him. She was riding side-saddle and wearing a very smart riding-dress with a high-crowned hat.

He dismounted and came around to her and held up his arms and she slid down into them. Their horses began to crop the grass.

'Still love me?' he asked.

'You know I do,' she said, turning her face up to his. He kissed her long and hard, and then said, 'The fact that your papa is on his way home is good news. We will get married the day he arrives.'

'So urgent,' she teased, leaning against him and hearing the steady beat of his heart against her breast. 'And do you know who my maid of honour is going to be?'

'Who, my sweet?'

'Why, Miss Pym, of course.'

'Excellent. Does she know?'

'Not yet,' said Deborah. 'But I have her address and I will write to her and ask her. And Abigail has written to me. We are invited to her wedding and we shall go for her sake, shall we not?'

'I would go to the ends of the earth with you,' said the earl, holding her close.

'Pretty, but hardly original,' said Deborah.

'My poor brother is still afraid of you. He crept in during the night and collected his finest clothes, or so Silvers tells me. I have a feeling he has gone to stay with Aunt Jill with a view to courting Miss Carruthers.'

'Poor Miss Carruthers.'

'Do not be too hard on William. I miss him.'

'Do you miss your old wild life? There is no need to be Miss Prim and Proper with me.'

Deborah laughed. 'Whatever gave you the idea I had turned prim and proper?' And she set to kissing him in a way that made his senses reel.

'Come along,' he said at last. 'I am close to forgetting we are not wed and there is no Miss Hannah Pym here to stop us!'

*　　　*　　　*

Benjamin walked a few paces behind Hannah and Sir George the next day in the gardens of Thornton House, making great play with his walking-stick and admiring the way the sun glinted off the silver top.

How boring gardens were, thought Benjamin idly. All stupid flowers and dull trees and bushes. But Miss Pym seemed enchanted. But then, anything Sir George said or did would enchant her.

Something would have to be done. Benjamin's shrewd black eyes rested on the pair: Sir George, elegant and courteous,

201

and Hannah breathlessly hanging on every word.

Benjamin had no thoughts of leaving his mistress, but he considered life was going to be uncomfortable if he were ever left alone in the country with a pining Hannah Pym. A married Hannah would stay in London with all its shops and taverns and amusements. A Hannah who had given up hope would go to that cottage in the country. Benjamin could picture it vividly—stone floors, rising damp, bad drains, or, more likely, no drains to speak of, bumpkins for company, and good works to pass the time.

Sir George would need a jolt in the direction of matrimony.

*   *   *

Mrs Courtney, like the rest of the polite world, learned from the newspapers that one Benjamin Stubbs, footman to a Miss Pym of South Audley Street, Stubbs who had trounced Randall at Rochester, had put up a splendid fight in Berkeley Square. Miss Pym? A footman? How could a servant afford a footman, of all creatures? Mrs Courtney quickly decided that Hannah must be some man's mistress. It was her duty to find out and relay such news to Sir George.

Benjamin noticed her haunting South Audley Street followed by her maid. He, in turn, followed Mrs Courtney, marked where she lived, and then waited until he saw the maid, Janet, emerge alone. Benjamin, with the fear of Lady Carsey still in his mind, wanted to make sure they were not being spied on by one of her friends.

He followed Janet for some distance, waited until she went into a shop, and when she came out, pretended to bump into her.

'I beg your parding,' he said. 'That I should harm such beauty.'

Janet giggled and then recognized Benjamin as being the footman of that woman her mistress had been trying to find out about. So when Benjamin pressed her to take a glass of ale with him, she readily agreed.

Benjamin quickly found out that Janet's mistress was a Mrs Courtney and that Mrs Courtney was interested in Sir George and therefore in Miss Pym. Benjamin deftly flirted and flattered the maid, plying her with drink, while his busy mind thought out how to turn this to Miss Pym's advantage.

'You see,' said Janet confidingly, 'I may as well tell you the truth, for Mrs Courtney is an old cat. She is furious because Sir George was seen out with this Miss Pym who she says is nothing more than a servant. She reads about you being Miss Pym's footman and decides some rich man is keeping Miss Pym and that Sir George should know about it.

Benjamin had a bold idea. If it did not

work, and Miss Pym ever found out about it, she would never forgive him. But then, there was the fear of that dreadful poking hole in the country that she might take him to.

He grinned. 'Mrs Courtney ain't going to like this,' he said. 'Is she a great gossip?'

'The worst,' said Janet, round-eyed.

'You see, the gent wot is keeping my Miss Pym is Sir George himself.'

'Lawks!' cried Janet.

*　　　*　　　*

'You reek like a brewery,' snapped Mrs Courtney, when her maid returned.

'All in a good cause,' said Janet with a genteel hiccup. She related Benjamin's news while Mrs Courtney stared at her open-mouthed and then got out her book and carefully scored out Sir George's name. Sir George had dared to be rude to her, Mrs Courtney; nay, he had run away from her in the Park. He should be made to suffer.

It was a prime piece of gossip. The very best gossip. 'You are a jewel, Janet,' said Mrs Courtney, and with a burst of democracy added, 'a real friend.'

*　　　*　　　*

As Hannah Pym sadly began to pack her bags for a journey to York, for Mrs Clarence must be found and Sir George must have more stories, the buzz of gossip ran round and round London.

It was not to reach the ears of Sir George until Hannah was well on her way.

Benjamin heard the gossip from the other servants in the Running Footman, a pub hard by, and rubbed his hands.

Sir George would have to make an honest woman of Hannah Pym. Gossip was as damning as the real thing.

He whistled loudly as he went to pack his own bags until Hannah's voice from the other room shouted to him to stop and then she came in to remind him severely of the duties of a proper footman. 'And what are you grinning at?' she finished.

'I warn't grinning,' said Benjamin piously. 'I was thinking o' the Bible. Cast thy bread upon the waters. Well, I've just cast the whole bleeding loaf!'

'Benjamin,' said Hannah, shaking her head. 'Sometimes I think you are stark, staring mad!'